"*I thought all men hated seeing a woman in tears.*"

"Only when they feel unable to do anything about it, when they can't follow their instincts...."

"To follow their instincts and do what?" she asked him wryly, thinking she already knew the answer, but Mitch's response to her was nothing like what she had expected.

"To do this...."

His lips were already touching hers, slowly caressing them, so that they softened and clung, instinctively responsive to a message so subtle and intimate that Georgia herself barely registered it.

PENNY JORDAN was constantly in trouble in school because of her inability to stop daydreaming—especially during French lessons. In her teens, she was an avid romance reader, although it didn't occur to her to try writing one herself until she was older. "My first half-dozen attempts ended up ingloriously," she remembers, "but I persevered, and one manuscript was finished." She plucked up the courage to send it to a publisher, convinced her book would be rejected. It wasn't, and the rest is history! Penny is married and lives in Cheshire.

Penny Jordan's striking mainstream novel *Power Play* quickly became a *New York Times* bestseller. She followed that success with *Silver*, *The Hidden Years*, and *Lingering Shadows*.

Don't miss Penny's latest blockbuster, *For Better For Worse*, available in July.

Books by Penny Jordan

HARLEQUIN PRESENTS
1508—A FORBIDDEN LOVING
1529—A TIME TO DREAM
1544—DANGEROUS INTERLOPER
1552—SECOND-BEST HUSBAND

HARLEQUIN PRESENTS PLUS
1575—A CURE FOR LOVE
1599—STRANGER FROM THE PAST

Don't miss any of our special offers. Write to us at the following address for information on our newest releases.

Harlequin Reader Service
P.O. Box 1397, Buffalo, NY 14240
Canadian address: P.O. Box 603,
Fort Erie, Ont. L2A 5X3

PENNY JORDAN

Mistaken Adversary

Harlequin Books

TORONTO • NEW YORK • LONDON
AMSTERDAM • PARIS • SYDNEY • HAMBURG
STOCKHOLM • ATHENS • TOKYO • MILAN
MADRID • WARSAW • BUDAPEST • AUCKLAND

ISBN 0-373-11625-X

MISTAKEN ADVERSARY

Copyright © 1992 by Penny Jordan.

This edition published by arrangement with Harlequin Enterprises B. V.

® and TM are trademarks of the publisher. Trademarks indicated with ® are registered in the United States Patent and Trademark Office, the Canadian Trade Marks Office and in other countries.

Printed in U.S.A.

CHAPTER ONE

SHE was late. She always seemed to be running late these days, Georgia reflected tiredly, as she checked the traffic and then hurried across the road.

The problem was that she hadn't been able to park her car close enough to the agency who supplied her with the computer programming work she did at home, which meant she had had to walk right across town—not a very long way, but it all added extra time to her schedule, time she could barely afford to lose, time when she wasn't earning money, when she wasn't——

She checked herself with a small grim exclamation. She had a very strict rule which meant that, once she was out of the house and on her way to visit Aunt May, she did not allow her growing anxiety over money to show in any way which might alert her aunt to what was happening and so destroy the concentration that she so desperately needed if she was to get well.

If she was... There was no if about it, Georgia told herself fiercely. Aunt May *was* going to get better. Hadn't they said at the hospice only last week how well she was doing, what a wonderful patient she was?

Georgia stopped walking, her expression of stern concentration softening as she thought about her aunt. Her great-aunt, really: an indomitable lady of seventy-odd, who had stepped in and filled the gaping chasm left in her life when her parents were so tragically killed in a plane crash, who had filled her life and her world so completely and so lovingly, who had helped her to overcome the trauma of losing her parents, and who had brought her up so wisely and so caringly that she considered herself to be far better loved, far better understood, than many of her contemporaries. And even when the time had come for her to spread her wings, to leave school, and her home, to go on to university and from there to London and her first job, her aunt had encouraged her every step of the way.

Keen, ambitious, intelligent and adaptable: those had been only some of the compliments and praise Georgia had received as she climbed the corporate ladder, determinedly reaching towards the goals she had set herself. A real high-flyer was how others described her, and she had been proud of that title, single-mindedly telling herself that there would be time—once she was established in her career, once she had achieved all that she wanted to achieve, seen and done all she wanted to see and do—to take life at an easier pace, to think about a serious relationship with someone and perhaps about children of her own.

Of course she had still kept in touch with her aunt, spent Christmases with her, and some of her other holidays, encouraged her to come up to London for brief stays in the tiny flat she had bought in one of the prestigious dockland developments, unfortunately just when their price was at its highest . . .

Yes, she had seen her path so clearly ahead of her, with no obstacles in her way, nothing to impede her progress, and then the blow had fallen.

Having an unexpected few days extra leave with nothing planned, she had gone north to the Manchester suburb where she had grown up, and discovered the shocking truth of her aunt's illness. A 'growth'. A 'tumour'. So many, many different polite ways of describing the indescribable, but no real escape, no nice polite way of covering up what was actually happening.

She had taken extra leave, ignoring her aunt's insistent command that she return to London and her own life. With her aunt she had seen doctors, specialists, made hospital visits, and then, once all the facts were known, she had gone back to London—but not for long. Just for long enough to hand in her resignation and to put the flat up for sale—which went through, but at a price which had left her with no financial margin at all.

Then had come the move out here to one of her aunt's favourite small Cheshire towns, and the purchase of the cottage, with what had been a horrendously large mortgage even before the recent interest rate increases. The work she received from the agency, no matter how many hours she worked, could never ever bring in anything like the salary her skills had commanded in London. And now added to those other burdens was the cost of ensuring that her aunt could continue to receive treatment at the very special hospice, only a handful of miles away from the cottage.

Today, as she did every day and every evening, Georgia was on her way to see her aunt, to spend time with her, achingly conscious of how frail she was, frantically sick inside with anxiety for her, desperately praying that she would keep on fighting . . . that she would get better . . .

It was only with the discovery of her aunt's illness that Georgia had realised that without her she would be completely alone in the world. That knowledge had bred inside her an anguish, a fear, which she was totally at a loss to control. It was, moreover, an emotion which was totally out of place in an adult woman of close to thirty. Of course she loved Aunt May, of course she desperately wanted her to get better—but to experience this despairing, consuming sense of desertion and fear . . . What she was going through now was worse, far worse, than the emotions she had experienced when she'd lost her parents. She was, she sometimes thought, getting dangerously close to going completely out of control, to giving in utterly and wholly to the maelstrom of emotions threatening her.

And yet, until now, she had prided herself on being a sensible, mature woman, a woman not given to the wilder impulses of emotionalism. Yet here she was, virtually trying to make a bargain with the gods, feverishly begging for her aunt's recovery. And still, on some days, her very bad days, it seemed to her that, no matter how hard she willed it to be different, her aunt was slowly slipping away from her . . .

And now, if she didn't hurry, she would be late for visiting time. Her arms were beginning to ache with the weight of the paperwork she was carrying. The woman who ran the agency had looked askance at her when she had asked her for extra work. They had the work, plenty of it, she had told Georgia, adding that people as skilled and dedicated as her were hard to come by—but was she really wise to overload herself to such an extent?

Georgia grimaced to herself. She needed the money and needed it desperately. The mortgage alone... When she had visited the building society last week, to see if there was any way of alleviating the crippling burden the mortgage had become, the manager had been sympathetic to her plight.

Had she thought of taking in a lodger? he had suggested. With a variety of new industries springing up locally, many of them offshoots of international concerns, there was a growing demand for such a service.

A lodger was the very last thing Georgia really wanted. She had bought the cottage for her aunt, knowing how much the latter had always dreamed of just such a quiet retreat, and she wasn't going to sell it or give up. Just as Aunt May wasn't going to give up her fight to hold on to life.

Tonight, before evening visiting time, she had someone coming round to see her—the prospective lodger she did not want. A male lodger at that. Not that the sex of the potential intruder made much difference; Georgia had lived in London for long enough to know that it was perfectly feasible for male and female to live together, sharing a roof, without there having to be any hint of a sexual relationship between them.

In fact she herself had been for a time the third member of just such a trio, and had found that, of her two co-habitees, Sam had been the easier to get along with. No, it wasn't her potential lodger's sex that put her off him, it was the necessity of having a lodger at all.

As the parish church bells rang out the hour, she suddenly realised that standing still was wasting precious time. Hurriedly, she stepped forward, almost cannoning into the man coming in the opposite direction.

As he took evasive action, so did she, thus beginning one of those familiar patterns of attempted avoidance of one another, so amusing to the onlooker and so time-consuming to the participants, whereby both of them, in trying to avoid the other, made the same move at the same time, thus prolonging the delay in what looked like some kind of complicated dance-step.

In the end it was the man who put an end to it, standing still and smiling ruefully as he suggested, 'Perhaps if I just stand still and you walk round me?'

He was a very tall man, and very well built as well, with broad shoulders and narrow hips, the kind of man who looked as though he either worked out of doors or engaged in some kind of outdoor physical activity. Certainly he was very fit, very lithe, because he moved easily and speedily, putting out a steadying hand as Georgia's impatience both with him and with herself boiled over, and her too tense body reacted to that impatience, almost causing her to stumble as she tried to avoid him.

His touch was brief and non-sexual, and yet it set off inside her the oddest of reactions, causing her to stiffen and look directly at him, unaware of the mixture of panic and anger flashing their twin messages from her eyes.

He was still smiling, a rueful curling of a very masculine mouth that matched the amusement in the sun-speckled golden eyes. He had a tan, the kind that came from being out of doors over a long period of time. His dark hair was thick, touched with gold where the sun warmed it.

He was good-looking—if you were the kind of woman who appreciated that kind of male machismo, Georgia acknowledged grudgingly. Personally, she had always preferred brains to brawn, and right at this moment she wasn't interested in either.

Irritated, and at the same time both defensive and vulnerable without knowing why she should be, instead of returning his smile with the friendly warmth it invited and deserved, she over-reacted, glowering at him, as she demanded grimly, 'Will you please let go of me and get out of my way?'

Later, five minutes down the road, still feeling hot and bothered, still anxiously aware of how much time she had lost, she waited for the lights to change so that she could cross the road to the car park, and she happened to turn round and catch sight of her own expression in a shop window. She was frowning: a cross, bitter expression pursed her lips, her body so tense and strained that she automatically tried to relax it.

She didn't, she recognised as the lights changed and she crossed the road, like the image she had just seen. It had shocked her into realising how much these last few months had changed her, draining her of her sense of humour, her optimism.

As she reached the car park, she remembered uncomfortably how she had reacted to the man in the street, someone who had cheerfully and pleasantly tried to turn a moment of irritation for them both into a light-hearted and warm exchange of good-humoured smiles. Her aunt would have been shocked by her behaviour to him; she had always stressed not just the importance of good manners, but the necessity of treating others with warmth and kindness. Her aunt was of the old school, and she had imbued in Georgia a set of values and a pattern of behaviour which was perhaps a little out of step with modern-day living.

Rather to her shame, Georgia recognised that her time in London, and the stress of the last few months, was beginning to wear down that caring attitude to others which her aunt had always believed was so important. Too late now to wish she had been less abrasive with that unknown man, to wish that she had responded to his pleasant good manners with equal good humour, instead of reacting so rudely. Still, she was hardly likely to run into him again, which was perhaps just as well: she hadn't missed the way his friendly smile had hardened a little when she had reacted so unpleasantly to him, to be replaced by a very grim look of cool withdrawal—of sternness almost.

*   *   *

Tiredly, Georgia unlocked her front door. The visit to the hospice had left her feeling drained and very, very afraid. No matter how much she tried to deny herself the knowledge, she could see how frail her aunt was growing, how terrifyingly fragile—so that in some odd way it was almost as though her very skin was becoming transparent. And yet at the same time she was so calm, so at peace with herself, so elevated almost, as though—and this was what terrified Georgia more than anything else—as though she was already distancing herself from her, from the world, from life...

'No! No!' Georgia bit her lip as she realised she had cried the protest out aloud. She didn't want to lose her aunt, didn't want...

Didn't want to be left alone like a child crying in the dark. She was being selfish, she told herself critically; she was thinking of her own emotions, her own needs, and not her aunt's...

All through the visit she had talked with desperate cheerfulness of the cottage and the garden, telling her aunt that she would soon be coming home to see everything for herself, telling her—as though the words were some kind of special mantra—about the cat who had adopted the cottage as its home, about the special rose bushes they had planted together in the autumn, which were now producing the buds which would soon be a magnificent display of flowers. Her aunt was the one who was the keen gardener, who had always yearned to return to her roots, to the small-town atmosphere, in which she herself had grown up. That was why Georgia had bought the cottage in the first place—for her aunt...her aunt, who wasn't living here any more, her aunt who...

Georgia could feel the ball of panic and dread snowballing up inside her and, as always, she was afraid of it, trying to push it down and out of the way, totally unable to allow it to gather momentum, to force herself to confront it. She was so desperately afraid of losing her aunt, so mortally afraid.

The cottage was only small: three bedrooms, one bathroom, and a tiny boxroom which she was using as her office, and then downstairs a comfortably sized living-kitchen area, a small cosy sitting-room and a dining-room which they never used, preferring the comfort of the kitchen. Its garden was large and overgrown: a gardener's paradise, with its rows of fruit bushes, its well-stocked borders, its small fishpond and its vegetable beds. But it was Aunt May who was the gardener, not her, and Aunt May——

Georgia swallowed the angry tears gathering in her throat as she remembered the look on her aunt's face when they had first come to look at the cottage. It had been that look of almost childlike wonder and pleasure which had pushed Georgia into taking the final step of committing herself to buy the cottage, even though she knew she could barely afford it. She had bought it for Aunt May. They had had nearly three months in it before Aunt May's health had started to deteriorate, before the doctors had started talking about a further operation, before it had become necessary for Aunt May to have far more intense nursing than Georgia could provide.

Refusing to allow what she knew to be tears of self-pity to fall, Georgia headed for the stairs, carrying the work she had collected. She knew without looking at it that it would keep her busy for the rest of the afternoon and for long into the night, but she didn't care. She needed the money if she was to keep on the cottage, and she had to keep on the cottage for somewhere for Aunt May to come home to when she was eventually able to leave the hospice. And she *would* leave it. She would come home. She had to.

Tiredly, Georgia went upstairs to the small boxroom which housed her computer. The cottage was old, and its loft space had been home to many hundreds of generations of house martins. The latest occupants scratched busily and noisily above her head while she worked. At first they had disturbed and alarmed her, but now she had grown used to the noise, and almost found it companionable. The cottage had originally been used to house agricultural workers, but had been sold off by its original owner, together with the land on which it stood. A prime site for development, the estate agents had told her. With so much land the cottage could be extended. Its privacy was virtually guaranteed, surrounded as it was by farmland, and at the bottom of a track which went virtually nowhere. But Georgia couldn't have afforded to extend it even if she had wanted to. She could barely afford the mortgage repayments, and then there was the cost of the hospice and her own living expenses, plus running the small car which was an absolute necessity now with Aunt May in the hospice.

Her head was beginning to ache, the letters on the screen in front of her beginning to swim and blur. She rubbed her eyes tiredly and glanced at her watch, unable to believe how long she had been working. Her whole body ached, her bones feeling almost bruised as she moved uncomfortably in her chair.

She had lost weight in these last few months, weight some might say she could ill afford to lose. She wasn't a tall woman, barely five feet five, with small delicate features that were now beginning to have the haunted, pinched look of someone under severe stress.

Her fair hair, which in London she had always kept perfectly groomed in a slick, neat hairstyle, had grown down on to her shoulders; she had neither the money nor the energy to do anything about getting it cut. The expensive London highlights had been replaced by the natural streaked effect of sunlight, just as her skin had gained a soft peachy warmth from that same exposure. She had never thought of herself as a particularly sensual or sexually attractive woman, but then she had never wanted to be, being quite content with the neatness of her oval-shaped face and the seriousness of her grey eyes.

She had her admirers: men who—like her—were too busy climbing the corporate ladder to want any kind of permanent commitment, men who, while admiring her and wanting her company, appreciated her single-minded determination to concentrate on her career. Men who respected her.

Yes, her career had been the sole focus of her life—until she had realised how ill Aunt May was. At first her aunt had protested that there was no need for her to go to such lengths—to give up her career, her well-structured life—but Georgia hadn't listened to her. It wasn't out of some grim sense of duty that she had made her decision, as one of her London friends had intimated. On the contrary, it had been out of love. Nothing more, nothing less— and there had not been one second of time since that decision had been made when she had regretted its making. All she did regret was that she had been so busy with her own life that she hadn't realised earlier what was happening to her aunt. She would never be able to forgive herself that piece of selfishness, even though Aunt May had reassured her time and time again that she herself had known about and ignored certain warning signs, certain omens, which should have alerted her to seek medical help earlier than she had.

The sound of a car coming down the bumpy track that led to the cottage alerted her to the arrival of her potential lodger. He was someone who apparently needed accommodation locally for a few months while he sorted out the financial affairs of a small local company his city-based group had recently taken over.

Georgia knew very little about the man himself, other than that the agency for whom she worked had been able to vouch for him as someone eminently respectable and trustworthy. When she had expressed doubts that someone as highly placed and wealthy as the chairman of a progressive and profitable group would want to lodge in someone else's home rather than rent somewhere, Louise Mather, who ran the agency, had informed her that Mitch Fletcher did not fit into the normal stereotype of the successful entrepreneur-cum-businessman mould and that, when he had approached her for help with the additional staff he needed to recruit, he had told her that all he needed was somewhere to sleep at night and where he would remain relatively undisturbed by the comings and goings of the other members of the household. For that he was prepared to pay very well indeed and, as Louise herself had pointed out when she had urged Georgia to think seriously about taking him on as a lodger, he was the answer to all her financial problems.

Wearily Georgia stood up, clutching the back of her chair when she went slightly dizzy. She had not, she realised, eaten anything since suppertime last night, and even then she had pushed away the meal she had made barely touched.

Perhaps the discipline of having to provide meals for a lodger might force her to eat more sensibly. In these last few weeks since her aunt had gone into the hospice, she had found preparing and then eating her solitary meals more and more of a burden. Some evenings, once she returned from her final visit of the day to the hospice, she felt far too drained of energy and emotionally wrought-up to bear to eat, and yet logically and intelligently she knew that she needed the energy that came from a healthy well-balanced diet.

She glanced out of the window and saw the car stop outside the front gate. A steel-grey BMW saloon, it looked sleekly, almost arrogantly out of place outside her humble home.

As she went downstairs she reflected that this Mitch Fletcher was probably writing the cottage off as unsuitable even before she opened the door. She did not, she acknowledged as she went towards the front door, really want the hassle, the responsibility, of sharing her home with someone else. She was afraid that the inevitable inroads it would make into her life would somehow threaten the need she felt to devote every second of her spare time either to being with her aunt or willing her to get better, to recover and come home.

When she opened the door the cool words of greeting and introduction hovering on her lips fled in disordered confusion as she recognised the man standing there.

As he stepped forward, Georgia recognised that, infuriatingly, she had somehow or other by her silence lost control of the situation—because it was he who broke the silence, extending his hand towards her and saying, 'Miss Barnes? Mitchell Fletcher. I understand from Louise Mather that you have a room you'd be prepared to let. I think she's explained the position to you: I'm looking for somewhere temporary to stay while I'm working in the area.'

As he spoke, he came forward, and Georgia discovered that she was stepping back almost automatically, allowing him to walk into the hallway.

Until he suddenly stopped, she hadn't realised that the shadows in her small hallway had cloaked her features from him, and that he had not, like her, had the benefit of that instant recognition.

Now, as he focused on her, she saw from his lightning change of expression that he had recognised her from their unfortunate encounter earlier in the day and, moreover, that he was not exactly pleased to be seeing her again.

His reaction to her brought all her earlier guilt and discomfort flooding back. Before, when she had so rudely ignored the brief moment of shared amusement he had offered her, she had comforted herself with the knowledge that they were not likely to meet again and that his awareness of her bad temper and unpleasantness was something that was unlikely to be reinforced by another encounter. But she had been wrong and, as she felt her skin flushing as the coolness in his eyes reminded her of just how unpleasant she had been, she had to subdue an extremely childish impulse to close the door between them and shut him out so that she wouldn't have to face that extremely uncomfortable scrutiny.

It seemed that he was waiting for her to speak and, since he had now stepped into her hall, she had no option but to at least go through the motions of pretending that this morning simply had not happened, and that neither of them had already made up their minds that there was simply no way they could ever share a roof...

'Yes, Louise has explained the situation to me,' Georgia agreed. 'If you'd like to come into the kitchen we can discuss everything.'

She had deliberately asked Louise not to mention her aunt or the latter's illness to Mitch Fletcher, not wanting it to seem as though she was inviting his pity.

Late afternoon sunshine flooded the comfortable kitchen. It was her aunt's favourite room, reminiscent, so she had told Georgia the first time they viewed the cottage, of the home she had known as a girl. On hearing that, Georgia had ruthlessly changed her mind about replacing the kitchen's ancient Aga with something more modern and getting rid of its heavy free-standing kitchen cupboards and dresser. Instead, she had done everything she could to reinforce Aunt May's pleasure in the room's homeliness—even if she did sometimes find that scouring the porous stone sink had a disastrous effect on her nails, and that the Aga, while giving off a delicious warmth, was not always as efficient as the modern electric oven she had had in her London flat. Maybe it was just that she was not accustomed to using it... Whatever, there had been several expensive mistakes before she had begun to appreciate its charms.

Once inside the kitchen, she waited, expecting to see distaste and scorn darkening Mitchell Fletcher's astonishingly masculine golden eyes as he compared the kitchen to the marvels of modern technology to which he was no doubt accustomed. To her surprise he seemed to approve of the room, stroking the surface of the dresser and commenting, 'Mid-nineteenth century, isn't it? A very nice piece too... Solid and well made. A good, plain, unpretentious piece of furniture without any unnecessary frills and fuss about it. Good design is one of my hobby horses,' he enlightened her. 'That's why——' He broke off. 'I'm sorry. I'm sure you don't want to hear my views on modern furniture,' he told her drily, adding in a more ironic tone, 'And I know you won't want me to waste too much of your time.'

She thought he was referring to her behaviour earlier in the day and could feel her face growing warm until he added, 'Louise did warn me that you would want to keep this interview short. In fact she stressed that you were looking for a lodger who made as few demands on your time as possible.' He was eyeing her in an odd way, with a mingling of cynicism and curiosity, as he asked her, 'If it isn't too personal a question, why exactly do you want a lodger?'

Georgia was too tired to lie and, besides, what did it matter what he thought? They both knew that he was not going to want to stay here. 'I need the money,' she told him shortly.

There was a brief pause and then he said wryly, 'Well, that's honest at least. You need the money, but I suspect that you most certainly do not want the company . . .'

For some reason his perception made her shift uncomfortably, almost as though a burr had physically attached itself to her skin and was irritating her, making her want to shrug off his allegation. 'As Louise told you, I don't have time to waste, Mr Fletcher. I'm sorry you've had an unnecessary journey out here, but in the circumstances I don't think——'

'Hang on a minute!' he interrupted her. 'Are you trying to tell me that you've changed your mind, that you don't now *want* a lodger?'

Georgia stared at him. 'Well, you can hardly want to lodge here...'

'Why not?' he demanded, watching her piercingly.

Georgia didn't know what to say. She could feel the heat scorching her skin, turning her face poppy-red. 'Well, the cottage is out of the way... and very small, and I expect... at least I assume——'

'It never does to make assumptions,' he interrupted her smoothly. Too smoothly, Georgia recognised uncomfortably. 'And if you think that I'm the kind of man to be deterred by what happened this morning... You don't have to like me, Miss Barnes—in fact to be honest with you the one thing that did tend to put me off was the fact that you are a young, single woman.' He ignored her outraged gasp, continuing silkily, 'I don't mean to condemn your whole sex for the silliness of a very small minority, but I'm sure you'll appreciate that, until meeting you, I was concerned that you might well be a member of that small minority——'

Georgia couldn't listen to any more. 'If you think that I'm looking for a lodger for any reason other than the fact that I need the money——' she began.

Without seeming to raise his voice, he cut through her angry demand to say coolly, 'Certainly not—now that I've met you. I'd like to see the room if I may, please...'

He wanted to see the room! Georgia stared at him. She had been so sure that he would not want to stay. She was *still* so sure that he wouldn't want to stay!

Angrily she led the way upstairs, opening the door into the spare bedroom. 'The cottage only has one bathroom,' she warned him curtly.

He had been looking out of the window at the garden. Now he turned round, looking very tall against the low slope of the dormer windows. He had been looking out at the garden and now, as he studied her, Georgia felt an uncomfortable *frisson* of sensation prickle warningly over her skin. This man would, she recognised with a small shock of unease, make a very formidable adversary.

An adversary? Why should she think of him in those terms? All she had to say was that she had changed her mind and that the room was no longer available, and he would be gone—safely out of her life.

'That's all right. I'm an early riser and likely to be gone by seven-thirty most mornings. Louise tells me you work from home?'

The question, so neatly slipped in under her guard, had her focusing on his face in surprised bewilderment, as though she were not quite sure where it had come from or why.

'Rather unusual in this day and age, to find a woman of your age and skills, living in such a remote spot and working from home...'

Something about the cynical way his mouth twisted while he spoke made her reply defensively, almost aggressively, 'I have my reasons.'

'Yes, I'm sure you do,' he agreed suavely.

Another shock skittered down her spine. He knew about her aunt, but how? Why? Surely——

'He's married, of course.'

Above her shock she was aware of the disgust, the anger almost in his voice, the condemnation held in the short flat statement that fell so shockingly against her ears.

'What?' Georgia focused disbelievingly on him.

'He's married. Your lover,' Mitch Fletcher repeated grimly, apparently misreading her reaction. 'It isn't so hard to work it out, you know: you live alone, you're obviously tense, anxious, on edge. You're out most evenings, so Louise tells me.'

He thought she was having an affair with a married man! Georgia was stunned. How on earth . . . ?

'He obviously isn't wealthy otherwise you wouldn't need to consider taking in a lodger. Don't you ever stop to think of the consequences of what you're doing—not just to his wife and family, but to yourself as well? The chances are he'll never leave her for you. They rarely do. And what satisfaction any woman can get from having to share a man with another woman . . .'

Georgia couldn't believe what she was hearing, and yet, to her astonishment, instead of denying his allegations, she heard herself responding bitingly, 'Well, since you so obviously don't approve, it's obvious that you won't be wanting to stay here.'

'I may not *want* to, but I don't seem to have much option. Finding lodgings around here is like prospecting for gold in the North Sea! I'd like to move in tomorrow if that's OK with you. I'm prepared to pay the full three months' rent in advance.'

Georgia had been on the verge of telling him that she had changed her mind, but now abruptly she stopped. Three months' rent in advance! She did a quick calculation and was astounded to discover how much money that actually was. Enough to cover the cost of her aunt's expenses and to help with the mortgage . . . She wanted to refuse—ached to do so in fact—but she couldn't let her pride stand in the way of providing Aunt May with all the comfort and care she could give her.

Swallowing hard on the impulse to tell him that his money was something she neither wanted nor needed in her life, she forced herself to say flatly, 'Very well, then, if you're sure.'

'I'm sure.' His voice sounded equally flat, hard and cold, unlike the warmth she had heard in it earlier in the day. He was walking towards her, and for some reason his easy cat-like tread made her retreat nervously on to the landing . . .

She was being ridiculous, she told herself as she headed for the kitchen. Just because he had jumped to a totally erroneous and unfounded assumption about her . . . an assumption she had deliberately chosen not to correct . . . Why hadn't she corrected him? Because she had been too shocked to do so? Had her behaviour been governed more by self-defence and shock than by a deliberate need to foster the antagonism between them?

Tiredly, she put a hand to her forehead, disconcerted by her own thoughts, guiltily aware that for virtually the first time since they had moved to the cottage she had allowed someone else other than her aunt to dominate her mind.

As she walked into the kitchen, he was right behind her, and yet when she tensed and turned round, he stepped back from her, as though he had sensed her feeling of uncertainty and being somehow overpowered by him—as though he was deliberately allowing her space, cooling down the heat of mutual antipathy which she had quite distinctly felt. As he stepped back he reached inside the jacket of his suit and removed a cheque-book.

Nervously Georgia licked her lips, a habit left over from her childhood which she had thought she had long ago brought under control. Once he had written that cheque—once she had accepted it from him—it would be too late to say that she had changed her mind. Yet, as she watched him, she could not bring herself to utter the words which would have banished him from her life...

When he had written the cheque he straightened up. Georgia left it where it was lying between them on the kitchen table. As she turned her head, she saw the time and immediately realised she was going to be late for seeing her aunt. Instantly everything else was forgotten, a strained, hunted expression tensing her face as she said quickly, 'I have to go out. I...'

'Such a devoted lover!' he mocked her sardonically. 'Is *he* equally devoted? I wonder... Do you ever think about the woman—the family—he steals the time from that he spends with you? Do you ever put yourself in her shoes? Do you?'

The cheque was still on the table. Angrily Georgia picked it up, her voice shaking as she held it out to him and said, 'You don't have to stay here.'

'Unfortunately I do,' he told her curtly. 'As I said, lodgings aren't easy to come by round here.' Ignoring her outstretched hand and the cheque, he turned towards the door. 'Until tomorrow evening, then... Would seven o'clock suit you?'

Seven was the beginning of visiting time. Shaking her head, she said quickly, 'Six would be better, or later—say about ten?'

Raising his eyebrows, he commented acidly, 'He spends as much time with you as that, does he? His wife must be a saint—or a fool...'

Too concerned about being late to see her aunt, Georgia didn't waste time on any response, simply going to the back door and opening it for him. As he came towards her she felt herself pulling in her stomach muscles, instinctively avoiding any kind of physical contact not just with him but with his very clothes. He paused as he drew level with her, looking thoughtfully at her for a moment so that it was impossible for her to avoid the deep scrutiny of his narrowed gaze.

'His wife isn't suffering alone either, is she?' he said quietly. 'You know, I can never understand women like you; to waste so much emotional energy and in such a worthless cause...'

'What would you know about it?' Georgia challenged him, driven to give in to the impulse to defend herself even while her mind screamed at her that she must get rid of him and get on her way to the hospice.

'A good deal. My father had a succession of mistresses before he finally divorced my mother to marry one of them. I saw the hell he put her through, and us. I grew up hating those other women for taking him away from us, until I realised that my father was the one I should really hate, and that they were just as much his victims as we were.'

His quiet admission left Georgia too astounded to make any kind of response—and then he was gone, walking round the corner of the cottage, heading for the front gate and his car.

CHAPTER TWO

'YOU'RE very quiet, Georgy. You're not still worrying about me, are you?'

Georgia focused on her aunt's pale face, forcing herself to try to smile. She had in fact been thinking about Mitch Fletcher and his extraordinarily intimate disclosure just as he was leaving the cottage. She really would have to tell him that he was mistaken about her, to explain—if not everything, then at least enough for him to understand that it was her aunt who took up so much of her time and not some non-existent married lover.

She frowned a little, acknowledging how hard it must have been for him to witness the disintegration of his parents' relationship, to have his own love for and trust in his father destroyed, as it obviously had been destroyed. Poor little boy... She caught herself up, shaking her head angrily. What on earth was she doing, feeling sympathy for someone who had suggested that she...? She bit her lip in vexation, unwillingly acknowledging that if he had misjudged her it was at least partly her own fault.

She wasn't really sure why she was so reluctant for him—for anyone—to know the truth. Was it because in facing their concern and sympathy she would be forced to make herself confront the reality of how seriously ill her aunt was? No... no!

Her thoughts scattered, frantically fleeing from what she could still not bring herself to face—fleeing from the enormity of that realisation... Her aunt *was* getting better... Only this morning she herself had said how well she felt, and yet as Georgia looked at the tiny figure in the bed, her fear was like cold, cold fingers tightening around her heart.

Unwillingly she looked into her aunt's face and saw the tiredness there. She was holding her hand and it felt so frail, so cold.

'Georgy——' her aunt smiled at her through her tiredness '—you mustn't ... you mustn't——'

She stopped speaking and, before her aunt could finish what she had been about to say, Georgia began to tell her about the garden, describing for her the new flowers that were opening, her voice high with denial of her terrible fear. 'But you'll be seeing them for yourself soon. Just as soon as you get well enough to come home...' She thought she heard her aunt sigh. Certainly the pressure of those frail fingers holding her own tightened a little. She could feel herself starting to tremble, as fear and love rolled through her.

As always, the precious time she was allowed to spend at her aunt's bedside was gone all too quickly, and it was time for her to leave. The sister in charge came towards her as she was going. Georgia smiled at her, saying eagerly, 'Aunt May seems so much better since she came here. I've been telling her about the garden. She's always wanted a proper garden of her own. The roses will be out soon. We bought them last year—scented ones. Perhaps she'll be home in time to enjoy them and——'

'Georgia, your aunt is doing very well,' the sister interrupted her. 'But you must realise——' She had to break off as one of the nurses came quickly towards her, excusing herself to Georgia as she turned aside to listen to what she had to say. 'Oh, dear, I'm afraid I'm going to have to go, but...'

As she watched her hurry away, Georgia fought to ignore the tension and fear she was feeling. Sometimes when she talked to her aunt about the garden, about the future, Aunt May looked at her with such a compassionate, concerned expression that Georgia felt as though... As though what? As though Aunt May knew and accepted something which she herself did not know—or did not *want* to know?

She was trembling when she got into her car, cold with fear.

As always when she suffered like this, Georgia found the only way to hold the terror and the pressure of her own despairing thoughts at bay was to work as hard as she could, so that all her mental energy was exhausted, making it impossible for her to dwell on the truth that her intelligence told her existed but which her heart refused to acknowledge.

It was almost one o'clock in the morning before she admitted that she was so tired that if she didn't stop working she would probably fall asleep where she was.

She had, she confessed to Louise Mather, been lucky to find an agency with enough work to enable her to temp from home, but Louise had corrected her, telling her frankly, 'No, I'm the one who's lucky to have such a highly qualified and hard-working person on my books, and if you ever *do* want something more permanent, don't hesitate to let me know.'

Louise knew what had prompted her move from London, but she was one of the very small circle of people who did. The doctor was another, plus the staff at the hospice, and the farmer's wife—who was their closest neighbour and who, in the days before Aunt May had gone into the hospice, had been a regular visitor, bringing them fresh eggs and vegetables, and shared with Aunt May her own countrywoman's lore. Aunt May was a very private person, and she had brought Georgia herself up the same way, and besides... Georgia leaned back in her chair, rubbing her eyes to relieve the strain of staring at the screen, and acknowledged that one of the reasons she was so reluctant to discuss her aunt's illness with others was because somehow in doing so it was as though she was physically holding it at bay, refusing to allow it to tighten its grip on their lives. It was as though, by refusing to admit its existence, she could somehow pretend that it did not exist. Was that what she was doing? she asked herself. Was that why she preferred to allow someone like Mitch Fletcher to believe that she was having an affair with a married man rather than admit the truth?

Mind you, if *she* had a psychological problem, then so too did he. How on earth had he managed to leap to the conclusions he had about her on such flimsy evidence? It hadn't been so much a leap as an impossible connecting together of facts which surely even a fool could see could not possibly amount to what he had seen in them. It was obvious that the trauma of his childhood had left a very deep impression on him—just as hers had left her with a fear of being alone, without someone she could call her own. Was that why she was so desperately afraid of losing her aunt? Not so much for her aunt's sake, but more selfishly for her own?

Georgia shivered, hugging her arms around her body as though trying physically to ward off the darkness of the thoughts passing through her mind. It was because it was so late... because she was so tired... because she was alone... Because she was still even now suffering the after-effects of the emotions churned up by Mitch Fletcher...

Mitch Fletcher. She stood up unsteadily, smothering a yawn. She should never have allowed him to give her that cheque. She should have stood her ground and told him that she had changed her mind, that she no longer wanted a lodger. But then that would not have been true: she did not want a lodger, but she *needed* a lodger because she desperately needed the income having one would bring in. What she did not want was a lodger in the form of Mitch Fletcher, and what was more she suspected he was perfectly well aware of her feelings. Despite the easy charm, the warmth she had seen so clearly exhibited earlier in the day when he had responded with humour to their small confrontation, there was quite obviously another man beneath that easygoing surface, a tough, determined man whose relaxed outward pose cloaked a will of steel. She shivered, acknowledging that it wasn't the cool night air coming in through her bedroom which was responsible for the lifting of the tiny hairs on her skin.

It was only when she was finally sliding gratefully into an exhausted sleep that she remembered that she hadn't told her aunt about Mitch Fletcher. Tomorrow, she would tell her tomorrow. No, it would be today now, she recognised in a confused manner, impatiently blaming Mitch Fletcher for the fact that, infuriatingly, although she was both mentally and physically exhausted, as soon as he had slipped into her thoughts all desire to sleep had somehow evaded her.

As she was discovering more and more often these days, her sleep was brief and not very relaxing, and her first thoughts when she opened her eyes were, as always, for her aunt. Perhaps her inability to sleep properly lately was a legacy of those weeks when her aunt had herself been unable to sleep and when she, Georgia, had—ignoring the protests— sat up with her, talking to her and trying to help her to overcome the intensity of her pain. Now her aunt was receiving the benefit of the hospice's care and experience in helping people to control and live with such pain, but Georgia herself could not get back into the habit of sleeping deeply and well.

Long before seven o'clock she was up and had eaten her breakfast—or rather had attempted to eat her breakfast, pushing away her cereal barely touched. Now, as she wandered through the garden, ignoring the discomfort of the early-morning dew soaking into her trainers, she paused to study the buds on one of the rose bushes she and her aunt had ordered the previous autumn. These were special roses, old varieties which they were growing for their scent rather than for the perfection of their blooms. As she looked at them, carefully examining them for any signs of greenfly, her throat ached with the pressure of the tears she dared not allow herself to cry.

When she returned to the kitchen for a pair of scissors and a basket and carefully cut a half-dozen or so buds, it was an impulse decision, and one which made her hands shake with emotion when she carefully placed the buds into the basket. Why was she picking them when surely her aunt would soon be able to come home and see them for herself? What was her subconscious mind trying to tell her? For a moment she was almost tempted to destroy the buds, to trample them into the ground, so that she could forget that strong current of awareness that had compelled her to cut them; as though some deep part of her was already acknowledging that her aunt would never see them blooming in their natural setting. A sharp, agonising dart of pain shivered through her. No... that wasn't true! As she tensed her whole body, bracing it to reject the strong current of her own thoughts, she saw someone walking across the grass towards her.

It took her several seconds to recognise Mitch Fletcher, and then several more to pull herself together sufficiently to wonder what he was doing.

She hadn't been expecting to see him until this evening.

He, like her, was wearing a pair of trainers, hence his unheralded approach. He was also wearing a dark-coloured tracksuit, and he explained briefly, 'I run this way most mornings, and when I saw you were in the garden I thought I'd stop to ask you if you minded if I brought my stuff round this after-noon instead of this evening? The hotel need my bedroom and they'd like me to check out before lunch...'

As she mentally calculated the distance from the town's one decent hotel to the cottage, Georgia reflected that it was no wonder he looked so tautly muscled and fit if he ran that kind of distance most mornings.

A lot of people used the footpath that went past the cottage to the farm, both for walking and running, and she had become so used to them going past that she scarcely noticed them now, hence the reason she had not spotted him before. His abrupt intrusion into her sombre and painfully reflective mood left her feeling jarred and on edge, exposed somehow, and anxious for him to go, and yet somehow still too saddened by what she had been thinking to make a snappy quick response to his question.

There was no reason why he shouldn't move in during the afternoon: she would be at home after all, working, and yet she wanted to say no to him. Did she want him lodging with her? She had no option now, and it would be stupid to allow her own emotions to cut her off from such a valuable source of much-needed income. She had kept from her aunt her worries about their financial resources, wanting the older woman to concentrate all her mental energy on fighting her cancer, not worrying about her niece.

'Old-fashioned shrub roses. My grandmother used to grow them.' The bleak, almost hard comment broke through her guard. She focused on Mitchell Fletcher as he leaned forward to examine the nearest bush.

Something in his voice made her question, 'You didn't get on with her?'

The look he gave her was sharp and prolonged. 'On the contrary,' he told her, 'she was the one source of stability during my childhood. Her home, her garden were always somewhere I could escape to when things at home got out of hand. She was my father's mother, and yet she never took his side. I think in many ways she blamed herself for his promiscuity, his lack of loyalty. She had brought him up alone, you see: her husband, my grandfather, had been killed in action during the war. She found great solace in her garden, both for the loss of her husband, and for the faults of her son. She died when I was fourteen...'

Unwillingly, Georgia felt her emotions responding to all that he had not said, to the pain she could tell was cloaked by the flat hardness of his voice. 'You must have missed her dreadfully.'

There was a long pause, so long that she thought he must not have heard her, and then he said even more flatly, 'Yes, indeed. So much so that I destroyed her entire rose garden... A stupid, pointless act of vandalism which incurred my father's wrath because by doing so I had seriously brought down the value of the house, which was by then up for sale, and caused another row between my parents.

'My father was in mid-affair at the time—never a good point at which to annoy him. We could chart the progress of his affairs by his moods, my mother and I. When a new one started, there was a general air of bonhomie and cheerfulness about him. As the chase hotted up and the affair began to develop, he would become euphoric—almost ecstatically so when the affair eventually became a physical reality. After that would follow a period when he was like someone high on drugs, and woe betide anyone who in any way, however inadvertently, came between him and his need to concentrate exclusively on the object of his desire. Later, in the cooling-off period, he would be more approachable, less obsessed. That was always a good time to get his attention.'

Georgia listened in silent horror, wanting to reject the unpleasantness of the words being delivered in that flat, emotionless voice, knowing how much pain, how much anguish they must cover, unwillingly finding herself in sympathy with him.

Abruptly he shrugged, a brief flexing of his shoulders as though he was actually throwing off some burden, his voice lighter and far more cynical as he added, 'Of course, as an adult, one realises that no one partner alone is responsible for all the ills in a marriage. I dare say my mother played her part in the destruction of their relationship, even though as a child I was not aware of it. Certainly what I do know is that my father should never really have married. He was the kind of man who could never wholly commit himself to one single woman...'

He leaned forward and looked into her basket. 'Roses... A gift for your lover?' His smile was very cynical. 'Haven't you got it the wrong way round? Shouldn't he be the one giving you roses, strewing them dew-fresh across your pillow in the best of romantic traditions? But then of course I was forgetting he can never be here for you in the morning, can he? He has to return to the matrimonial pillow. I'm not surprised you want to keep this place. It's ideal as a lovers' retreat: tucked away here, cut off from the rest of the world, a secret, secluded, private paradise. Do you ever ask yourself about her—about his other life, his wife? Yes, of course you do, don't you? You couldn't not do. Do you pray for him to be free, or do you pretend that you're content with things as they are, gratefully taking the small part of his time that is all he can give you, believing that one day it will be different—that one day he will be free?'

'It isn't like that,' Georgia protested angrily. 'You don't——'

'I don't what?' he interrupted her. 'I don't understand? Like his wife? How your sex does love to delude itself!' He turned away from her. 'Will it be all right if I come round this afternoon with my stuff, or will it interfere with...with your private life?'

'No, it won't,' Georgia told him furiously. 'In fact——'

'Fine. I'll be here about three,' he told her, already starting to lope away towards the gate, with the easy movement of a natural athlete.

Impotently, Georgia stared after him, wondering why on earth she hadn't acted when she had had the opportunity and told him not only just how wrong he was in his assumptions but also that she had changed her mind and that she was no longer willing to have him as a lodger. Too late to wish her reactions had been faster now. He had gone.

The perfume of the roses wafted poignantly around her. She touched one of the buds tenderly. Poor boy, he must have been devastated when he lost his grandmother. She could well understand the emotions which must have led him to destroying her roses...the grief and frustration. He must have felt so alone, so deserted. It was so easy for her to understand how he must have felt. Too easy, she warned herself as she walked towards the house, reminding herself that it wasn't the boy she was going to deal with but the man, and that that man had leapt to the most erroneous and unfair assumptions about her, based on the most tenuous of links and such scant knowledge of her.

Later, as she showered and prepared for her visit to her aunt, her conscience pricked her, reminding her that she needed only to have stopped Mitch Fletcher when he first mentioned her supposed lover and that she ought to have corrected him then. Why hadn't she done so? Not because she was the kind of person who enjoyed allowing others to misjudge her so that she could wallow in self-pity and then enjoy their embarrassment once the truth was ul-

timately revealed. No, it wasn't that. It was because... because she was afraid of discussing her
aunt's condition with anyone, afraid... afraid of
what? Of what she might be forced to confront in
doing so?

Her heart had started to hammer, the familiar
feeling of panic, despair and anger flooding through
her, the sense of outrage and helplessness... Abruptly she switched off, refusing to allow her
thoughts to charge heedlessly down the road they
were heading—down a road she could not allow
them to go. Why? Because she knew that road led
nowhere other than to an empty wasteland of
anguish and pain. She had, after all, already trav-
elled down it once when her parents died. Then
there had been Aunt May to help her, to hold her,
to comfort her. Now there was no one. No, she
would be completely on her own...

She could feel the panic building up inside her,
the rejection of what her mind was trying to tell
her, the impotent rage and misery.

As she went downstairs she saw the roses she had
cut, and for a moment she was tempted to pick them
up and throw them into the dustbin. Then she remembered Mitch Fletcher's flat and yet extraordinarily graphic description of his destruction of his
grandmother's rose bushes and she quelled the
impulse.

CHAPTER THREE

'Roses—oh, Georgy, you shouldn't have! They must have been so expensive.'

Georgia looked at her aunt's downbent head as she breathed in the perfume of the opening buds, and told her quietly, 'No, I picked them from the garden, from the roses we planted last autumn. I meant to make a note of which bush they were from, but M... someone interrupted me and I forgot.'

'From the garden...'

Her aunt put down the roses and turned to look at her. There was such an expression of love and understanding in her eyes that Georgia felt her own fill with tears. Holding out her arms to her, her aunt said gently, 'Oh, Georgia, darling. I know how you must feel, but you mustn't... you really mustn't... We've so little time left, you and I, and I want us to share it, not to——'

She stopped as she heard the anguished sound Georgia made.

'No! That isn't true!' Georgia protested. 'You *are* going to get better. I——'

'No, Georgia, I am not going to get better,' her aunt corrected her, holding her tightly, her voice steady as she lifted her hand to push the hair back off Georgia's face. 'Please try to understand and accept that. I have, and I can't tell you how much

43

peace, how great a sense of awareness of all the good things I've enjoyed about my life...how deep a feeling of being at one with the rest of the world it has brought me. Of course there are times when I feel despair...fear, when I want to deny what's happening—to protest that it's too soon—but those feelings are fleeting, a bit like the tantrums of a child, who doesn't really know *why* it protests— only that it feels it must. My one great fear has been for you. My poor Georgia... You've fought so hard to ignore what we both know to be the truth. I've watched you and hurt for you, and yet, at the same time as I've wanted to protect you from what must happen, I've wanted to share it with you—to show you how easy, how very natural what's happening to me is. That's one of the things they teach us here: to let go of our fear, to share what we're experiencing, to accept its——'

'Its inevitability?' Georgia questioned her brokenly, struggling with her tears and with the turbulent anger of her emotions, knowing she wanted to deny what her aunt was saying—to tell her that she must not give up, that she must continue to fight—and yet conscious at the same time of her aunt's need to talk about what was happening to her and to share it with her. They talked for a long time, her aunt's awareness and acceptance of what lay ahead of her both humbling Georgia and causing her the most intense fear and grief.

'Thank you for sharing this with me, Georgy,' her aunt said softly to her, when she finally admitted how exhausted their talk had left her. 'So many people find that long, long after they have come to accept that their lives are drawing to a close, and that death can be something they can accept without fear, their relief in discovering this is offset by their family's and friends' refusal or inability to share that knowledge with them. It is a very natural fear after all, the fear of death, and in western civilisations it's a fear that is strengthened by the taboo surrounding the whole subject of death. I want to share this with you, Georgy. Selfishly, perhaps. I know what you went through when you lost your parents...'

'I'm afraid of losing you,' Georgia admitted. 'Afraid of being alone...' As she spoke the words, the emotions she had been fighting so hard to control overwhelmed her, and with them came the tears she had not previously allowed herself to cry, seeing them as a sign of weakness, of defeat.

When she finally left her aunt's bedside, she told herself that she was finally coming to accept that her aunt's life was drawing to its end, and yet she knew that, deep within her, one stubborn childish part of her was still protesting, objecting, begging fate to intervene and to arrange a miracle for her. For *her*, she noted inwardly—not for her aunt, but for *her*.

She had spent far longer than usual at the hospice and, when she finally got back to the cottage in the middle of the afternoon, the first thing she saw was Mitch Fletcher's car parked outside. He himself was seated inside it, a briefcase on the seat beside him, while he was apparently engrossed in some paperwork.

'I'm sorry,' she apologised shortly. 'I . . . I was delayed.' The trauma of the morning had made her virtually forget that she had agreed he could move in earlier than they had originally arranged, her guilt adding to the already heavy burden of negative feelings he seemed to arouse inside her.

'No problem,' he told her easily. 'As you can see, I've managed to keep myself fairly well occupied. That was something I ought to have asked you, by the way: I do tend to bring work home with me—something they weren't too keen on in the hotel. Do you mind?'

Georgia started to shake her head, knowing that, the more time he spent occupied with his business affairs, the less she was likely to see of him. 'As you know, I work at home myself, sometimes in the evening as well as during the day.'

He paused in the act of getting out of his car, giving her a thoughtful, ironic look, which immediately changed to a frown as he focused properly on her. 'Been giving you a bad time, has he?' he asked her drily.

For a moment she didn't know what he meant and then she realised he thought she was late because she had been with her lover. The irony of the gibe made her want to weep. If only he knew where she had been . . .

Even now her throat still ached from her tears, and her senses still felt bludgeoned by the numbing pain of what she had had to confront. No matter how often she told herself that she must not be selfish—that she must give as generously and lovingly to her aunt as the latter had always done to

her, that now was her opportunity to repay her aunt
for all the loving support Georgia herself had received from her over the years—she still wanted to
howl like a child and protest that her aunt could
not be dying, that she must not leave her. And yet
even now, despite everything that her aunt had said
to her, she still could not bring herself to be open
about what was happening, to risk sharing it with
someone else... to explain to Mitch Fletcher just
where she had been.

Instead she had responded with terse flippancy.
'What makes you think that?'

He was out of the car now, standing virtually in
front of her, and as she started to turn away from
him he reached out, stopping her, his hand cupping
the ball of her shoulder, so that she could feel the
warm pressure of his grip through the thinness of
her blouse. The shock of it stilled her where she
was. She wasn't used to such a powerful male touch,
and as she stood immobile beneath it it struck her
that it had been a long, long time since her life had
included any kind of intimacy with a man, especially the non-sexual kind that came from having
male relatives and friends. Her youthful exper-
iments with sex had led her to the conclusion that
it was a vastly overrated activity, and in her life
since then there had not been the time or the space
to develop an intimate one-to-one relationship.
During her university days she had had her fair
share of male friends and admirers, had known then
the familiarity of a casual expression of affection
and fondness. But just how much her body had
become her own private territory, and how unused

she was to sharing any kind of physical proximity with others, was brought home to her by the almost violent *frisson* of sensation that raced over her skin, causing her muscles to clench in rejection as she froze on the spot, unable to draw away as he reached out with his free hand and gently touched her face with his fingertips.

The words, 'You've been crying,' seemed to reach her through a long canyon of echoing sound, distancing her from reality and separating her from the warmth of the sun on her skin, the familiarity of her surroundings, so that she was overcome by an almost terrifying surge of weakness. Her whole body started to tremble violently as, without any kind of warning at all, tears started to flood her eyes and roll down her face.

She heard Mitch Fletcher curse, but the words barely registered. The intensity of her grief was so overwhelming that there simply wasn't room for her to feel anything else. She was aware of him releasing her, and of the way her body started to shake, her self-control torn apart by her physical reaction to the morning's trauma.

Totally out of the blue, she was lifted off her feet, and she reacted instinctively, clinging on to him as Mitch carried her towards the house. She could hear him saying something to her, but the words were meaningless.

'Your keys, Georgia. Where are your house keys?'

Slowly the words sank in. She opened her hand, showing him the keys she was holding and letting him take them from her. She still held her balance against his body as he opened the door.

Once inside, the hallway was a blur of darkness that she could see only dimly through her tears. She was still crying, still trembling with the force of her emotions. Too caught up in reliving what she had learned to be really aware of what was happening to her, she was carried into the kitchen and eased gently into the chair in front of the Aga.

As he released her, she heard Mitch demanding roughly, 'What the hell has he done to you?'

She stared at him in confusion, and he added tersely, 'Why do you let him put you through this? Why do you allow yourself to be hurt and used? What did he do? Tell you he can't see you any more? Tell you his wife won't let him go, or that he can't leave her because of the children?'

Slowly the words started to penetrate. Slowly and painfully, like a child learning to read, Georgia repeated them to herself, until at last the sense of what he was saying to her sank in properly. 'No, you don't——' she began, her tears stopping as she realised what he was thinking.

But instead of letting her go on he interrupted her almost savagely, saying, 'Even now you still try to defend him! Even now when he's reduced you to this state, you'll still say that you love him and that he loves you and that all that's keeping you apart is his wife and his loyalty to her. Can't you *see*——?' He broke off, shaking his head, then bitterly answered his own question. 'No, of course you can't . . . or won't. If I told you that probably all he wants you for is the adrenalin boost you give him —

the excitement of having illicit sex—you'd deny it immediately. If I said that it was probably sexual desire that motivated you, you'd be horrified and claim that you love him. And yet how can you? How can anyone love someone who has quite plainly shown themselves unworthy of that love by the very fact that they're already breaking their marriage vows? How can you claim to love someone whom you probably don't even really know, someone whom you'll never really get a proper chance to know?'

'This has nothing to do with sex,' Georgia denied vehemently, standing up to confront him across the small space that divided them.

'You mean that as yet you haven't been lovers,' he hazarded, totally misunderstanding her, leaving her floundering in an astounded silence as he added, 'I must confess I find that very hard to believe. You don't need me to tell you that you're a very desirable woman, with the kind of subtle sensuality that's always much more of a turn-on than something more blatant. You have that aura about you that compels a man to think about what a pleasure you would be to love.'

'To have sex with, don't you mean?' Georgia corrected him acidly, overcoming her discomfort. It was a shock to hear him describing her in such an unfamiliar way. She had never thought of herself as either particularly desirable or sensual, and something odd and disconcerting quivered uncertainly inside her in response to his words.

She watched as he frowned and looked away from her, pressing home her point as she added grimly,

'After all, according to you, sex is all that any man would want from me.'

'Not *any* man,' he corrected her, turning back to look at her. 'And I certainly didn't mean to imply... I was just trying to point out to you that a man who is unfaithful to his wife with you is just as capable of treating you, and your feelings, with the same callous disregard.'

'I don't happen to agree with you. Many divorced men and women go on to have extremely happy and faithful second marriages.'

'Some do,' he corrected her, 'but very rarely with the person they initially left their spouse for. Is that what you're hoping for?' he asked her drily. 'That he will leave her and marry you?'

Reaction was beginning to set in. Georgia discovered that she was trembling not just with the shock of the morning's events, but with the realisation of how deeply enmeshed she was becoming in a tangle of totally idiotic untruths. If she tried to extricate herself from it now, she suspected that Mitch Fletcher would be unlikely to believe her. The irony of that knowledge made her check a hysterical desire to laugh.

'If you really want some advice,' Mitch told her roughly as she started to walk away from him, 'don't cry in front of him. Married men hate it when their lovers give them a hard time emotionally.'

'I thought all men hated seeing a woman in tears,' Georgia commented tiredly.

'Only when they feel unable to do anything about it, when they can't follow their instincts . . .'

Georgia was virtually on a level with him now. Luckily before she went out she had made up the bed in the room he was going to occupy, but she needed to get some towels out of the airing cupboard for him, and perhaps if she busied herself with such mechanical and mundane physical tasks it might help her to bring her chaotic thoughts to some kind of order.

'To follow their instincts and do what?' she asked him wryly, thinking she already knew the answer. The male sex was very good at removing itself from the scene of female emotionalism, but Mitch's response to her was nothing like what she had expected.

At first when he moved towards her she simply stared at him in confusion, not understanding what was happening even when he said huskily to her, 'And do this . . .'

His fingers were touching her face, gently rubbing away the final damp traces of her tears. His head was bending towards her, his breath sending tiny *frissons* of awareness skittering across her skin, so that her lips parted instinctively on a tiny murmur of denial.

But it was already too late. His lips were already touching hers, slowly caressing them, so that they softened and clung, instinctively responsive to a message so subtle and intimate that Georgia herself could barely register it. She only knew what her senses dictated and that was that she move closer towards him, that she let her muscles soften and her body relax, that she let the sense of comfort and pleasure which was lapping through her gather strength and momentum, that she allow herself to experience the delicate intensity of sensation she could feel when his fingertips brushed her skin, and his lips caressed hers.

It was years since anyone had kissed her like this, with such gentle thoroughness, such indulgence and care. In fact her blurred mind could not remember a time when anyone... She gave a tiny shudder as the slightly rough pads of his fingertips stroked over her throat. Her eyes were closing, her body nestling instinctively closer to his, welcoming its warmth, its strength, its power to hold her safe from everything that threatened her. She made a tiny sound of contentment, unaware of the shocked reaction tensing Mitch's body as he hesitated and looked down into her face.

He had never meant...never intended... He had been so angry with her, so helplessly aware of the futility of what she was doing, and yet now, in his arms, she was making him feel as though he was the only man...

He took a deep breath, breaking the kiss, forcing a distance between them so that Georgia opened her eyes, chilled by the loss of contact with his body, achingly wanting its return—its warmth. Confused, she looked up at him, and then, as she saw the coldness, the rejection in his eyes, she realised what she was doing, quickly pulling herself free of him, her face scarlet with humiliation and embarrassment. Until he'd touched her, she hadn't known how desperately, how deeply she ached for someone to lean on: someone to share her grief with, someone to love and support her. Someone... but not specifically this man, she assured herself as she turned her back on him, saying fiercely, 'It's too late for me to change my mind now, I know, but if you ever, *ever* do anything like that again, then I shall have to ask you to leave.'

'Don't worry, I shan't,' she heard him responding in a clipped hard voice. And as she went upstairs, she knew shamingly that, of the two of them, *she* was the one who was more to blame, she the one who—even if she had not initially invited his kiss—had quite unmistakably, and to her mind unforgivably, responded to it. And not merely responded to it, but actively, urgently wanted it. And wanted him?

No, of course not. That was impossible. Why should she want him? He was a stranger, and someone moreover who had given her every logical reason to dislike him. So why had she experienced in his arms that overwhelming sense of comfort and security? Why had she felt so responsive to him, so aware of him in the very deepest sensual way?

Shaking her head, as she tried to dispel questions she knew she could not answer, she opened the airing cupboard door.

A couple of hours later, when, having settled himself into his room, Mitch announced that he was due back at the factory and that he would not be returning until much later in the evening, Georgia couldn't hide her relief. Perhaps she had lived alone for too long? she reflected, as she heard him leaving. Despite the fact that she had flat-shared a great deal in her late teens and early twenties, Mitch's presence in the cottage was making her feel extraordinarily on edge and ill at ease. It had even managed to take her mind off her aunt. And yet there was no reason for her to feel like this.

She and Mitch Fletcher had had a brief businesslike discussion about the way in which his presence in the cottage would dovetail with hers. He would organise his own meals, he had told her crisply, and they would include breakfast, and sometimes an evening meal—but not always, as his group's takeover of the local company meant that he dined out a good deal with a variety of business colleagues. He had also reaffirmed that he would be bringing work home with him and that, when he was in in the evening, he would be working upstairs in his room. 'Just in case you were concerned that my presence might disturb your private life,' he had added, causing her to glare angrily at him.

At his suggestion she was going to draw up a rota for the bathroom, so that there were no awkward clashes of who used it and when. From the schedule he had outlined to her, it seemed that he was going to be up and out of the house well before her normal getting-up time, which meant that there would be no problem there. If at first she had wondered why a man of his age and very obvious physical appeal should still be unmarried, once she had thought about the punishing work schedule he seemed to set himself she no longer did so.

Did he always work such long hours, she wondered, or was it simply something that had happened because of the takeover? She hadn't realised—until Louise Mather had corrected her misconception—that Mitch wasn't merely an employee of the main company but that he was its founder and major shareholder and obviously a very wealthy man. And yet he seemed to have scant regard or need for the sybaritic kind of lifestyle she had assumed such a man must lead, and certainly there had been no suggestion that while he was lodging with her she should be responsible for providing his meals or doing his laundry. He seemed to accept it as a matter of course that these should be his own responsibility.

All in all, in many ways he sounded like an ideal lodger; and the cheque she had paid into the bank for his rent had certainly taken a good deal of the pressure off her too slender finances.

Really, when she thought about it, she admitted a little guiltily, the money he was paying her—for what was really merely the use of a bedroom and bathroom—was not just generous, but almost excessive. And she knew that, had her aunt been here, she would have insisted on providing him with far more cosseting than she, Georgia, was prepared to offer.

But then why should she cosset him, she asked herself angrily, after the way he had misjudged her... the way he had treated her? She suppressed the sharp twinge of guilt that reminded her of just how she had felt when he kissed her. If she closed her eyes now, it would be the easiest thing in the world to remember just how she had felt... just how she had...

Crossly she forbade herself to give in to such a dangerous temptation: she had work to do before visiting time. Visiting time! Her heart seemed to tremble physically inside her, the familiar urge of panic and pain drowning out her determination to keep her own feelings at bay and to concentrate on what her aunt must be feeling, on giving her the support and love she needed. She had to put her aunt first and not herself.

Frantically she rifled through the papers on her desk, knowing that only by immersing herself in her work was she going to be able to blank out her anguish.

The first thing that struck her later that day when she walked towards her aunt's bed was the scent of roses; the second was how fragile, and yet at the same time how at peace with the world, her aunt looked in those first unguarded seconds before she realised that Georgia was there. Emotional tears stung Georgia's eyes as she came to an abrupt halt in the middle of the ward, seeing so plainly now what she had refused to see before: that in her own selfish need, her own despair, her own love, she had in many ways been placing an additional burden on her aunt's shoulders—that she had been forcing her to live the lie she had been telling herself, namely that her aunt would get well.

As she stood there, a feeling of deep sadness and guilt filled her. She didn't hear the ward sister's approach and had no awareness that she was there at her side until the sister touched her arm, saying softly, 'Georgia...'

When Georgia turned her head, starting a little, she saw in the sister's eyes both knowledge and sympathy.

'Your aunt told me that the two of you had had a long talk. I'm so glad. One of the hardest things we have to deal with here is helping patients' relatives to accept that someone they love is approaching death... Over and over again we hear from the patients themselves how intensely they need to share what they're feeling with those they love, and yet are unable to, because their family and friends cannot accept, as they themselves have learned to accept, that they are approaching death.

'So many times they tell us how positive they feel, how strong... how much they want to die with strength and dignity, and how often they feel unable to communicate this to those closest to them, because of their refusal to accept what is happening. I know how much it means to your aunt to be able to share her feelings with you.'

'I've been such a coward,' Georgia told her, 'and worse, I've been selfish as well—refusing to even let her tell me what she's been feeling, what she does feel. You see, she's all I've got and, selfishly...'

'I know, Georgia. She's explained to me how she brought you up after your parents' death. There's no need for you to feel ashamed or guilty about your own feelings. Just because we're adults, it doesn't mean that we no longer feel all the emotions we felt as children, and alongside all the positive emotions—the love, the empathy, the caring and concern—there will be times when you'll feel anger, resentment—even hatred isn't uncommon.'

'You mean I could start blaming Aunt May for leaving me the way I did my parents when they were killed?'

'Exactly,' the sister agreed. 'Hard as it is for our patients, and it *is* hard for them—very, very hard sometimes—it can be even harder for those who love them. For our terminally ill patients we can provide all the care, all the medication, all the counselling and concern that they need to help them both physically and emotionally to control and govern the manner of their dying. But for those who love them we can do nothing to ease the burden of grief that death will bring.'

As she glanced down the ward towards her aunt's bed, Georgia said emotionally, 'I still can't really believe it. I was so sure she was going to get well . . . She's always been so strong, so positive.'

'Then help her to continue to be strong now, Georgia. Help her to approach the end of her life with that same courage.'

As though alerted by some sixth sense, her aunt suddenly lifted her head from her pillow and turned to look down the ward. As she saw how weak she was, Georgia's heart ached. This evening she was seeing her without the scales of self-deception; her aunt was, she could see, very, very weak, and very, very frail, and yet for weeks now she herself had wantonly ignored that weakness and frailty and had coerced her aunt—out of love and concern for her—to expend far too much of her meagre physical resources in bravely pretending that she was recov-

ering. As tears blinded her, Georgia cursed herself
for her selfishness and made herself a vow that from
now on she would put her aunt's needs first and
not her own.

'You look tired,' her aunt commented, as Georgia
sat down next to the bed. 'You work far too hard.
That mortgage is far too much of a burden for you,
Georgia. I blame myself...'

She was worrying the edge of the sheet with her
fingers as she spoke. She was plainly fretting, her
concern as always for her niece, Georgia thought
guiltily as she took hold of her aunt's hands, no-
ticing as she did so how tiny and shrunken they
were, how fragile and thin the flesh covering the
delicate bones.

'Well, don't. I love the cottage just as much as
you do, and as for the mortgage—I've taken in a
lodger...' She went on to explain what had happened, omitting to tell her aunt about Mitch
Fletcher's misconceptions about her, omitting
everything that would make her aunt think she was
anything other than idyllically happy with the
arrangement.

She didn't realise quite how over-generous she
had been in her praise, until her aunt commented
happily, 'Well, I can't tell you how relieved I am
that you aren't living there alone any more. I know
it's old-fashioned of me and I suppose you were
far more at risk living in London, but the cottage
is isolated, and it's a great relief to me to know that
you've got such a charming and reliable man living
there with you. I feel so guilty about the way you've

given up your career—everything—because of me, and now——'

'Don't!' Georgia interrupted her. 'There's no need for you to feel like that. In fact——' she paused, squeezing her aunt's hand, and then took a deep breath before beginning to say comfortingly '—I'm finding that I actually prefer living in the country, and the slower pace of life. I like the independence of being my own boss, so to speak. I enjoy being able to stop work if I feel like it and to go outside and spend an hour or so in the garden.' And she discovered, as she said the words, that they were actually true, and that she simply did not miss London and her high-powered career in the least.

'So, a-afterwards...you'll stay on in the cottage?'

Afterwards... It took her several seconds to realise what her aunt meant and, when she did, she had to stop herself from automatically denying what she was saying, swallowing back her words, reminding herself of her vow to put her aunt first. 'Providing the mortgage rate doesn't go any higher,' she answered wryly.

'If you do stay, it would be nice if you built that pergola we talked about over the winter. I just imagine it in the summer smothered with the rose we liked—*"Félicité et Perpétue"*, I think it was called.'

Fresh tears stung Georgia's eyes. She felt her aunt's hand tremble in her own and saw that she too had tears in her eyes.

It was a very emotional visit, and afterwards, too wrought up to go straight home and back to the work waiting for her, she parked the car in a quiet lane and got out to go and lean over the farm gate and absorb what comfort she could from the time-lessness of the landscape.

It was growing dark when she eventually walked back to her car, her body stiff and sore. She had, she realised, been standing motionless for over an hour, and now the softness of the early summer evening was cloaking everything with lavender-grey veiling.

As she switched on the car's headlights and drove home, she had virtually forgotten that Mitch Fletcher even existed, and it came as a distinct shock to draw up outside the cottage and see the lights on inside. The last thing she wanted at the moment was to have to deal with any other human being, but most especially with one of the calibre of Mitch Fletcher.

CHAPTER FOUR

To GEORGIA'S relief, when she unlocked the back door and walked inside, the kitchen was empty. She put down her handbag and started to make herself a cup of coffee, acknowledging vaguely that she really ought to have something to eat, even as her stomach revolted against the very thought of food. Perhaps later, she told herself, as she picked up her cup of coffee and headed for the stairs and her small office.

She could see a line of light under the door to Mitch's room, but she neither paused nor stopped outside it, if anything increasing her walking pace to carry her more quickly past it. She opened the door to her study and switched on the light.

The programming she was doing was highly complex, requiring intense concentration. As she worked, her coffee grew cold and was forgotten. She often had to pause to blink her tired eyes before refocusing on the small screen in front of her. Once or twice she had to stop work to smother a yawn, but she still kept on working, despite the weight of exhaustion pressing down on her. Very soon now there would be whole days and nights when she could not work, when she would be very glad of the cheque Mitch Fletcher had given her.

But then later—afterwards—there would be all the time in the world for working, all the time in the world for... She swallowed, the lump of panic and despair filling her throat, reminding herself of her vow to be strong, to put her aunt first. It might be weeks, it might be a month or even two, but no longer, the sister had warned her. She started to shiver as the darkness of her fear engulfed her.

In his bedroom, Mitch put down the papers he had been studying and glanced at his watch. It was almost one in the morning. He stood up, stretching until his bones cracked, acknowledging that he had probably worked too long, but then the solitude and peace of the cottage was conducive to concentration, unlike the hotel in which he had been staying.

He had heard Georgia return, and had been tempted to go downstairs on the pretext of making himself a drink, just so that he could... So that he could what? Try to make her see sense about the destruction her affair was going to cause, not only in her own life... Or had that simply been an excuse? For a moment, when he had held her in his arms... Stop being a fool! he taunted himself roughly. She was in love with another man, and, no matter how strongly he might feel that her married lover was deceiving her, using her, she obviously felt very differently.

What was he like, he wondered bitterly, the man who while committed to another woman still felt free to lie and cheat his way into her heart? And *he* would have been the one to institute the affair, he knew that instinctively. There was too much vulnerability, too much sensitivity about her for her to have deliberately and cold-bloodedly set about the seduction of a married man.

Mitch was an intelligent man. He didn't need anyone to tell him how deep and lasting an effect his own parents' marriage had had on him. It had given rise not only to his revulsion against the hypocrisy and shallowness of men who cheated on their commitments, but also to a reluctance within himself to allow himself to fall in love, at least during his twenties. Since reaching his thirties that reluctance had given way to an awareness of a need within himself to share his life with someone, to build up a secure relationship which included children as well as a lover and companion. He was, he recognised, something of an idealist, perhaps seeking an ideal which could not exist. There had been the usual experimentation when he was younger, followed by a very intense and short-lived affair with a fellow graduate which had ended when she had opted for a career in America. Since then there had been women in his life, friends rather than lovers, odd dates arranged with a variety of intelligent and attractive women whose company he had enjoyed but whom he had no real desire to see again, and it disturbed him to have to acknowledge how very intensely and sexually he was responding to Georgia. Because she was unavailable? If there was no other man in her life, no lover...how would he feel then?

The immediate and very intense way his body responded physically to such a suggestion stunned him. He frowned, wondering if it might not be better for him to look for somewhere else to stay.

If he felt like this now, how was he going to cope with the enforced intimacy that sharing a roof was bound to cause? Look at the way he had seized upon the flimsiest excuse today to touch her, to kiss her, even when she had made it more than clear to him that she was involved with someone else!

He was too tense to sleep, he decided as he opened his bedroom door and stepped out on to the landing. The door to Georgia's bedroom stood open. It was dark inside, and he could see that the curtains were still open and the room unoccupied. As he stood on the landing he could hear the quiet hum of her computer. A light shone underneath the study door. He frowned: she was working even later than he was. She had been in virtually all evening. What had happened? Had her lover let her down? Was she trying to find solace, to escape into her work? It was a lonely life being the other woman. He knew that from his father's relationships: some of his women, driven to despair by his callous treatment, had actually resorted to coming to the house and burdening his mother with the outpourings of their feelings. How on earth she had endured the marriage for as long as she had, he really had no idea. It was something they had never discussed, and now it was too late. Before her death he had wanted to ask her why she had stayed, but she had always been a very private person, not given to confiding in others.

He went downstairs to the kitchen and started to make some tea—enough for two people. He made some sandwiches from the supplies he had brought with him earlier, again more than he knew he wanted to eat, even though he had not actually acknowledged yet why. The easiest thing for him to do would have been for him to eat his supper in the kitchen, but instead he put it on a tray and took it back upstairs with him.

It was only when he was once more back on the landing, studying the betraying strip of light under Georgia's study door, that he thought about what he was doing. He rapped briefly on the door, and then when there was no reply he pushed it open.

The light was full on, the computer humming quietly away, but Georgia was oblivious to her surroundings. She was deeply asleep, her body contorted by the angle of her chair, her head pillowed on the arm she had rested on her desk. When she woke up she would be as stiff as hell, Mitch realised, and she'd be lucky if her arm didn't seize up with cramp. She must have been exhausted to have fallen asleep like that. He frowned as he looked at her, wondering how her lover could let her work herself into such a state. Didn't he care about what she was doing to herself—about what he was doing to her? The first time he had seen her, in the street, he had been struck by her tension, her slenderness, and if she worked like this all the time, it was no wonder.

As he stared at her, she jerked suddenly in her sleep, her eyes opening, her whole body tensing as she recognised him and struggled to sit up...

Georgia blinked rapidly. Her eyes felt gritty and sore, her head ached, and she was desperately thirsty. As she struggled through the numbing layers of sleep, she was acutely conscious of Mitch Fletcher standing silently watching her. How long had he been there? She shivered a little, filled with a very normal human dislike of the vulnerability of knowing he had watched her while she herself was unaware of his presence.

'I saw a light on under the door,' she heard him saying. 'I'd been downstairs to make myself a drink. I thought you might like one.'

She focused briefly on him. He was wearing jeans and a thin cotton shirt, the sleeves rolled back to reveal his forearms. They were tanned and leanly muscled, covered in fine dark hairs. An odd weakening sensation spread through her, making her tremble and her stomach muscles clench against her physical response to him. It was something new to her, feeling this physical awareness of a man in such an intense way. She had never dreamed, never imagined that it was possible to be so sensually responsive to something as mundane as the sight of a man's forearm. Women, in her experience, did not get turned on by the sight of the male body, despite feminine jokes about the effect of a very masculine backside covered by a pair of well-fitting denims, but she couldn't deny the way her body was reacting now.

It was all too easy to imagine touching his skin, running her fingertips along his arm in the most delicate and sensitive of caresses, feeling his muscles clench, knowing that he was going to reach for her and kiss her, knowing that when he held her he would understand the effect he was having on her. She closed her eyes quickly, trying to blot out his image, and with it her appalling sensual fantasy, but the darkness simply intensified what she was feeling. Beneath her clothes, she was intensely aware of the sensitivity of her skin, of the way the fabric covering it suddenly seemed to rub and scratch, so that she ached to be free of it, so that she ached to have the cooling balm of his hands moving slowly over her body...

'I made tea. I find coffee keeps me awake.'

The words seemed to float on the silence as though they belonged in a different world. She tried to cling to them, to use them to bring her back to normality. It was being in this room with him, she told herself frantically. It was the lack of air in the small space—she was suffering some kind of oxygen deprivation and that was what was responsible for her appalling thoughts...

She tried to get up, impelled to escape from the small room's intimate atmosphere, but as she stood up savage pins and needles numbed her left leg, so that she stumbled awkwardly and would have fallen if the desk hadn't been in the way. As it was, she couldn't help crying out at the pain of falling against the sharp corner of the desk.

Mitch had had his back to her as he poured the tea. Now he turned round, frowning in concern, putting down the teapot and coming towards her, taking hold of her upper arms before she could stop him, exclaiming almost roughly, 'Stay where you are, otherwise you'll probably end up with cramp.'

Stay where she was? She had no other option, since he was blocking her only exit. As it was, she was starting to tremble violently, not from the shock of the pain in her bruised thigh but because of her proximity to him.

The pins and needles in her leg made her wince and reach down instinctively to rub her leg, but to her shock Mitch stopped her, pushing her hand away as he said grimly, 'Better let me do that. You can barely stand up as it is. Why on earth did you keep on working when you must have known . . . ?' He stopped talking and dropped to his haunches in front of her. The sensation of his hand against her calf shocked her into complete immobility. His skin felt warm and slightly rough. It had been a warm day and her legs were bare, her skin pale and blue-veined.

As she stared at his downbent head in shocked disbelief, his fingers circled her ankle. Until that moment she had never realised how fragile or vulnerable she could feel, but now the sight of his fingers, lean and brown against her pale skin, made her shiver with a mixture of shock and fear. Not of him—her brain had already recognised that there was nothing remotely threatening in his touch, that he was simply reacting to what he had perceived as her need for help—no, her fear was of herself, of her own feelings, her own terror of being unable to control her reaction to him.

He was rubbing her calf now, a smooth rhythmic movement which was designed to bring relief from the pins and needles attacking her flesh, but which instead made her so intensely and sensually aware of him that she cried out automatically against her feelings, demanding sharply, 'Let go of me!'

He did so at once, standing up and looking grimly at her as he said with wry irony, 'I'm sorry. I was merely trying to help.'

Her own awareness of the illogical and unfair way she was behaving made her snap aggressively, 'Well, don't. I don't need your help and I certainly don't want it.'

His mouth tightened and a *frisson* of fear ran through her; she was pushing him too hard, being objectionable and aggressive, over-reacting in every way, in fact. She tensed, waiting for him to retaliate by reminding her of how she had responded to him earlier, but instead he simply said quietly, 'It isn't wise to work until you're so physically exhausted that you fall asleep where you're sitting, you know. Your tea's over there. If I were you I'd drink it and then go to bed, but then you don't need my advice, do you?'

He was gone before she could apologise for over-reacting or thank him for the tea he had brought her. And five minutes later, when her pins and needles had finally subsided and she was able to walk comfortably to her room, his bedroom door was firmly closed, even if the light showing underneath it proclaimed the fact that he himself was not yet in bed.

Oddly, for the first time in weeks Georgia slept deeply and well, waking up feeling more refreshed than she had felt in a long time. The house felt emptily silent and she knew even before she went downstairs that Mitch wasn't in it. It disturbed her, this atavistic awareness she had of him.

Like the bathroom, the kitchen was immaculate. He was, she reflected as she made her own breakfast, the perfect lodger—at least, he would be if only... If only what? If only she wasn't so physically and sensually aware of him. That was her fault and not his: he thought she was the mistress of a married man, and he had made it more than plain how he viewed the participants in such a relationship.

She pondered for a while on what he had told her about his own upbringing. Illuminatingly, and against her will, she had a startling mental image of him as a child, golden-eyed, serious-faced, trying to hold back his tears and fight down his fear as he witnessed his parents' quarrels. He must have had a very unhappy childhood, she reflected, contrasting it with her own happy, secure upbringing and the love with which her aunt had surrounded her, and it was perhaps not surprising that he should disapprove so strongly of her supposed relationship with a married man. She was even beginning to understand why he had leapt to that completely unfounded conclusion on first meeting her...

She gave a faint sigh as she glanced round her immaculate kitchen. Had she secretly been hoping that he would turn out to be so untidy and without thought for the fact that the cottage was her home that he would give her an ideal logical excuse for asking him to leave? But if she did that she would have to repay the money he had paid her. And that was something she simply could not afford to do.

She knew from the questions Aunt May had been asking her that the older woman was very, very anxious about her niece's future and her ability to meet the financial burden of the mortgage, and since it seemed she could do nothing else for her, Georgia reflected unhappily, she desperately wanted to give her aunt peace of mind where she herself and her future were concerned. The last thing she wanted now was for her aunt to be burdened by worry for her. No, it seemed as though she was stuck with Mitchell Fletcher, no matter how much she wished she weren't.

Later, when she went upstairs to her office, she noticed that the door to Mitch's bedroom was closed. She paused outside it without really realising what she was doing, appalled to discover that she had taken a step towards it and that she was actually about to put her hand out towards the door-handle...

What on earth had she been intending to do? she asked herself with horror as she quickly spun round and walked into her office. Surely she couldn't really have intended to intrude on his privacy and go into his room, knowing that he wasn't there? She gave a small shudder of self-disgust, wondering if she was in danger of developing the worst kind of obsessive, unpleasant traits, prying into another person's material possessions when he wasn't there to prevent it. She had no idea what had drawn her so compulsively towards that closed door, and what was more she had no desire to find out what might have drawn her. Hadn't she got enough on her plate right now without allowing herself to be vulnerable to any kind of emotional or physical involvement with a man, and especially with a man like Mitchell Fletcher, who had already made it plain what he thought of her and her morals?

The trouble was, she admitted half an hour later as she got ready to go to visit her aunt, that her emotions were so unstable at the moment, so much in danger of see-sawing wildly out of control because of what was happening to her aunt, that she seemed unable to exercise her normal cool self-restraint. It was almost like shedding a protective outer layer of skin, leaving herself far too vulnerable, far too responsive to situations, people and events in a way that was totally unfamiliar to her.

Georgia had to break her journey to the hospice to call in and see Louise Mather to hand over some work she had completed for her. The older woman welcomed her warmly, inviting her to join her for a cup of coffee. Over the coffee, Louise enquired sympathetically as to how her aunt was progressing. The familiar lie was on the tip of Georgia's tongue when abruptly she realised what she was doing: she had been deceiving herself for so long, terrified of admitting to the truth, that the fiction of saying that her aunt was doing well and getting better was an ingrained habit. A habit it was time she broke, she told herself shakily.

Quietly she told Louise the truth, blinking away her tears as her friend responded with genuine sympathy and compassion. 'Aunt May is wonderful; she seems to have come to terms with what's happening, and she's so full of... of acceptance and love, and a tremendous—well, peace is the only way I can describe it. There isn't really a word...'

'I know what you mean,' Louise told her. 'It was the same when my grandmother was dying. She was ninety-one and, when I protested to her that she could live until she was a hundred, she told me that she didn't want to, that she was ready to die. At the time I was horrified—I couldn't understand what she was telling me. She'd always been such a fighter... I felt as though she had somehow turned her back not just on life but on us, as though she was rejecting us in some way. It took me a long time to accept and understand what she was trying to tell me, to realise how selfish I was being in not allowing her to share her feelings with me, in not allowing her to say what was in her heart. If you need anyone to talk to, Georgia, I'm always here...' Tears clogged Georgia's throat as Louise touched her arm lightly in a gesture of warmth and comfort.

'Tell me how you're getting on with Mitch,' Louise demanded, changing the subject. 'I must say I was really impressed with him. I'm getting marvellous reports from the temporary staff he's hired from us. Apparently he's an excellent employer, knows how to be tough when it's necessary, but is always scrupulously fair and prepared to listen. I must admit that I had qualms about one or two of the younger girls... I mean, he looks so incredibly sexy, and some of our younger girls are inclined to romantic flights of fantasy. But Helen, one of my best temps, who's in her fifties, tells me that he has the most marvellous and tactful way of dampening down that kind of youthful ardour without causing any hurt feelings or damaged pride. That's something I really admire in a man, when he's sensible enough not to be susceptible to that kind of flattery... In fact, Helen seems to have taken a rather motherly interest in him. She was complaining the other day to me that he works too hard. Apparently, there's a rumour going round the company that he might be considering moving his head office out here. It does make sense: at the moment it's situated just outside London, and I know from what he's said to me that he'd prefer a country base to one in the city. Has he mentioned anything to you?'

Georgia shook her head. 'We haven't discussed anything personal. In fact we'll barely see one another: he'll leave in the morning before I'm up, and both of us will be working in the evening. You won't say anything to him about Aunt May, will you?' she asked. 'I...I still haven't completely come to terms with what's happening yet myself, and...'

Immediately Louise covered Georgia's hand with her own. 'I do understand, and I promise you I won't say a word. I've got some more work for you, if you want it, but I don't want to overload you. I know the sort of stress you must be under, so if you want a breather...'

Immediately Georgia shook her head. 'No, it's better if I keep on working. It stops me from brooding, and besides... well, the mortgage rate isn't showing any signs of coming down, is it?'

'No,' Louise agreed. 'I know what you mean. We moved in the lull just before the storm, so to speak. So far we're coping—just—but we have friends who moved at the wrong time and are now having to think seriously about selling and moving down-market. That is, if they can find someone to sell to...'

They continued to chat for a few more minutes until Georgia announced that it was time for her to leave.

'Remember,' Louise instructed her as she accompanied her to the door, 'if you need someone to talk to, day or night...'

Thanking her, Georgia hurried on her way.

Determined to spend every possible moment with her aunt, Georgia discovered over the ensuing weeks that it was possible to live in the same house as someone and yet almost not know that he was there. Some days the only evidence of Mitchell Fletcher's occupation was the fragrant scent of coffee in the kitchen when Georgia came downstairs after he had gone. Like the elusive masculine cologne that scented the bathroom, she found it an unwanted trace of him that left her feeling uncomfortably disturbed and on edge. It was almost as though she wanted him to be there in person, rather than to leave these subtle, haunting reminders of his presence in her home in a way that she felt played far more dangerously on her subconscious senses than the actual physical reality of him could ever have done. A dozen or more times a day, she found herself thinking about him, mentally visualising him, wondering about him. A weakness which she quickly and very sternly checked.

One week went by and then another, and then three weeks after her aunt had first insisted that she accept the truth—that she was not going to recover from her illness—Georgia arrived at the hospice to discover that her aunt's condition had started to deteriorate.

There was nothing she could do, the staff told her gently, five hours later. Her aunt had been given the necessary medication to ease her pain and enable her to sleep, and their recommendation was that Georgia herself went home and did the same thing. Unsaid, but implicit in that suggestion, was the hint that this was the beginning of the end and that Georgia would be wise to sleep and strengthen her stamina while she had the opportunity to do so.

She had already discussed with her aunt and made plain to the staff that she wanted to be with her when she died and now, although she was tempted out of emotionalism to protest that she wanted to stay, she forced herself to remember that the dedicated and caring hospice staff knew what was happening far better than she did, and it would be sensible to follow their advice.

After bending to touch her aunt's face and gently kiss her, she headed for the door. It was gone six o'clock in the evening. They would telephone her immediately if there was any change in her aunt's condition, the sister assured her.

Tiredly Georgia drove home. A shower, something to eat, a return to the hospice and then an early night—that was what she needed, that would be the sensible thing to do.

Thankfully there was no sign of Mitch's car when she drew up outside the cottage. Wearily, she got out of her car and walked towards the back door. She was glad that she would have the cottage to herself. The last thing she felt like doing now was making even the most mundane and ordinary conversation with anyone, but much less with Mitch, against whom for some reason she always felt she had to be so much on her guard, so very, very defensive and protective of herself. And yet why? In what possible way did he threaten her? She hardly ever saw him, for one thing, even if she was absurdly over-conscious of his presence in the house, like someone with sensitive skin suffering the chafing of an over-rough garment, and yet there was no reason why she should feel like this. If anything, he was more protective of his privacy than she was of hers... All right, so he *had* kissed her—once—in anger... But that meant nothing and was something best forgotten. A momentary aberration, that was all.

She took off her jacket, leaving both it and her handbag on the kitchen table, and headed for the stairs. The hours of sitting at her aunt's bedside, coupled with the knowledge of what lay ahead of her, had drained her to the point of numbness. The realisation of what was happening had still not really sunk in; a merciful layer of blanketing exhaustion was cushioning her from that shock. Once upstairs, she headed automatically for the bathroom, turning the handle, and pushing open the door so that she could walk inside.

The realisation that Mitchell Fletcher was already in there came too late to halt her passage into the small room. He had obviously just stepped out of the shower, his body completely naked, droplets of moisture still coursing over his skin as he paused in the act of reaching for his towel. The total unexpectedness of seeing him there, when she had thought the house was empty, deprived Georgia of her ability to do anything other than stand there and stare, while her heart raced, and her mouth went dry.

Later she acknowledged to herself that what happened next was probably her fault, that if she hadn't been so thrown, so . . . so shocked and transfixed by the sight of him, if she had reacted much faster, and simply and immediately turned on her heel and left then . . . But she did not turn on her heel and leave. Instead she remained where she was, rooted to the floor, unable to take her eyes off his body, her gaze dazedly fixed on a droplet of water that rolled off his shoulder, gathering momentum as it found a pathway over the water-sleek hair on his chest, following that fine dark pathway down the flat tautness of his belly until . . .

Georgia gasped as she witnessed the physical and very masculine arousal of his body, too stunned to even think of looking away, never mind leaving the room. Her eyes widened, her body tensing, a wholly feminine awareness and responsiveness coiling the secret feminine muscles deep within her own flesh as she trembled in recognition of his maleness. Then she heard Mitch curse, and saw him reach for his towel, the abrupt discord of his movements bringing her out of her physical trance, giving her the impetus to move which she had lacked before, sending her turning awkwardly on her heel, so that she almost collided with the door as she rushed blindly out of the bathroom and into her own bedroom. There she stood trembling in front of the bed, hands pressed to her hot face, her eyes squeezed tightly shut as she tried to blot out the memory not just of what she had seen but of her own shocking reaction to it.

Why on earth hadn't he locked the door? What was he doing here? Where was his car? Why, oh, why hadn't she knocked on the door first? Why, when she had realised he was in there, hadn't she immediately turned on her heel, instead of...instead of gawping like a schoolgirl, witnessing her first sight of the male body, and helplessly, fascinatedly transfixed by its differentness, its...its maleness? And as for her momentary physical reaction to his body... But no, she didn't want to think about that, didn't want to... She swallowed nervously and discovered that her stomach muscles were locked tightly against the errant ache of sensation inside her that wouldn't go away.

As she stumbled across the room, she caught sight of herself in the mirror and tensed in horror. Her face was flushed, her eyes glittering with an unfamiliar heat, her hair untidy from the pressure of her hands against her face, and as for her body... It was a warm day and she was wearing a short-sleeved T-shirt, fashionably loose-fitting, but it was still possible to see quite clearly the swollen thrust of her nipples where they pressed against the fine fabric.

Had she looked like that when she was in the bathroom? Had he...? She licked her dry lips, remembering the way she had stared at him, had followed the progress of that small bead of moisture, had...

Had it been because of *that* . . . because of *her* that his body . . . that he . . . ? She bit off a small strangled moan of anguish, unable to bear the thought that *she* might have been the one responsible for what had happened, and yet horribly aware that, once she was over the initial shock of discovering that she wasn't alone in the house, the sight of his naked body had not so much shocked her as held her in motionless, silent wonder . . .

'No!' The denial was ripped painfully from her throat, causing her to shiver violently. She heard the bathroom door opening and froze, staring at her closed bedroom door while her heart pounded— but it never opened. She remained where she was, virtually unable to move, all thoughts of the shower she had intended to take, the meal she had intended to eat, forgotten as she tried to quell the frantic race of her heartbeat. For over half an hour she remained in her room, before telling herself that she was behaving like a fool and that sooner or later she was going to have to face him.

CHAPTER FIVE

WHEN Georgia walked into the kitchen Mitch was already there, making some coffee. He turned round when she walked in, studying her in silence for so long that she could feel her heartbeat starting to race again and her face grow warm. She wanted, she discovered, to look everywhere but at him, and the effort of holding the gaze of those sombre golden eyes took every ounce of will-power she possessed.

When he asked her evenly, 'Want some coffee?' she almost wanted to laugh, so great was her feeling of tension. Instead she shook her head and then nodded, changing her mind, tempted by the rich smell of the freshly made brew.

As he poured her some, she heard herself saying almost apologetically, 'I thought you were out... I couldn't see your car,' half stumbling over the words, while inwardly she was cursing herself, telling herself that it wasn't her place to apologise but his. After all, he was the one who...

'It's being serviced. They're dropping it off for me first thing in the morning. I've got a dinner engagement this evening with a business colleague, and I came back to shower and change first. Like you, I assumed I had the house to myself.'

He sounded more rueful than apologetic, Georgia noticed, mentally reflecting on the difference between male and female attitudes. A woman caught

by a man as he had been caught by her would have
been deeply self-conscious and mortified by the experience, whereas he ... If either of them felt mortified, she suspected it was she, not so much because
of his nakedness but because of her own response
to it. A response which she desperately hoped he
had not registered.

He was walking towards her, causing her to flinch
back from him, so that a quick frown touched his
forehead as he put the coffee-mug down on the table
beside her and looked thoughtfully at her. She was
flushing again, she realised as, desperately looking
everywhere but at him, she felt the heat fill her face.

For a moment she thought he was going to let
her reaction go by without comment, but, just as
she was about to release a shaky breath of relief,
he lifted his hand and shockingly she felt the light
touch of his fingers against her hot face. Their
touch was cool, soothing almost, but she jerked
back from it immediately, her skin scorched with
heat as he said softly, 'Am I to take it that this is
because of what happened upstairs?'

She couldn't say anything...couldn't look at him,
angrily hating him for adding to her embarrassment by referring to it, that embarrassment
propelling her into demanding huskily, 'Surely you
must see——'

'I can certainly see why *I* might have felt embarrassed,' he agreed, interrupting her. 'But you're
a woman, not a girl, a woman moreover with a
lover...'

'And because of that I don't have the right to be
embarrassed by the sight of... by... by what hap-

pened? Is that what you're trying to say?' Georgia demanded, angry now at what she felt he was implying.

'Not that you don't have the right,' Mitch corrected her, 'and certainly I can understand why you might feel annoyed and offended by my...my physical reaction to you. It isn't your right to react to what happened that I was questioning. It was simply the *way* in which you reacted: your obvious embarrassment was something I hadn't expected. It threw me a little, I'm afraid, otherwise I would have followed you and apologised there and then. You rather caught me off guard. I thought I had the house to myself. Until you opened the door and walked into the bathroom, I had no idea... You looked as shocked as though...' He stopped when she flinched back as though he had physically touched her, frowning at her as he surveyed her flushed face and tense body.

'You *are* embarrassed, aren't you? You don't even like me mentioning what happened...and yet the sight of a male body can't be all that unfamiliar to you.'

'Why? Because I have a lover?' Georgia challenged him chokily. 'That's like saying that a sexually active woman has no right to be offended by the sight of a man exposing himself to her in the street...that a woman with a lover has no right to object to being raped——'

'Now just a minute: if you're trying to imply that I fall into either of those two male categories...' Mitch interrupted her sharply.

'I wasn't,' Georgia corrected him. 'But *you* were implying that because I have a lover I have no right to feel shocked by...'

'By what?' he asked her softly. 'By the sight of my *body*, or by my physical reaction to you? Which of them was it that shocked you so much, Georgia?'

She couldn't look at him. Her body felt as though it was a long slow burn of colour. She had never imagined when she came downstairs that he would talk to her intimately and frankly about what had happened. She had assumed that he would be as anxious to pretend nothing *had* happened as she was herself. She felt hunted, exposed... unable to retreat and incapable of responding with the sophistication she craved to have.

'You're a woman,' he continued. 'You must be used to the effect you have on men; the way they respond physically to you...'

Tiny nerves were jumping betrayingly under her skin. Deep within her body she could feel the most unnerving and unwanted reaction to what he was saying: a tiny sharp pulse of excitement and tension that made her lock her muscles in protest against its message.

'I don't want to discuss this any more,' she told him huskily. 'I... I have to go out.'

She turned her back on him, picking up her mug of coffee and heading for the kitchen door.

'What do you do when you make love with him, Georgia? Close your eyes?'

The sardonic words followed her, causing her to slop her coffee on to the floor as the shock of them coursed through her body.

'Hasn't he told you how very erotic a man finds it when a woman watches him making love to her, when she sees his response to him, when she admires his body and takes pleasure in the effect she has on it, instead of shutting her eyes, like a child taking a nasty dose of medicine.'

Georgia could hear the contempt in his voice, the anger almost, although what right he had to be angry with her she did not know. After all, she was the one who had . . . She swallowed hard, horrified to discover that tears were almost blinding her eyes as she searched frantically for the door-handle so that she could make her escape from him and rush back upstairs to the privacy of her own room.

Once there she tried to compose herself, but, every time she felt herself starting to relax a little, back would come the words he had said to her, accompanied by a far too clear and vivid mental picture of his naked body.

From her bedroom window she had a clear view of the lane, and it was only when she saw a taxi being driven along it and realised that it had obviously come to pick Mitch up for his dinner engagement that she finally felt able to go downstairs to the now thankfully empty kitchen.

Half-heartedly she started to prepare a meal for herself, but then the telephone rang and instantly she tensed, thinking it must be the hospital. When it wasn't, she discovered that the tension had destroyed her appetite so completely that all she could do was pick at the salad she had prepared for herself, before going back upstairs to get ready to return to the hospital.

It was only when she realised that she was delaying confronting the moment when she would have to walk into the bathroom and have her own shower that she recognised why.

Heat scorched her skin again as she gritted her teeth and forced herself to do so, firmly locking the door behind her before stripping off her clothes and stepping into the shower.

Once there, she paused in the act of soaping her body, remembering, without knowing how the memory had managed to slip past her guard, the sight and scent of Mitch's body. Faultlessly her own body responded to the stimulation of her mind and its memories, the effect so powerfully erotic that she gasped out loud in protest, standing rigidly still as she tried to deny what was happening to her.

What was wrong with her, behaving like this, reacting like this to a man whom she barely knew, and didn't even like? Angrily she scrubbed at her skin, wincing as she bruised her tender flesh.

She didn't want to remember how she had felt when she looked at Mitch's naked body, how she had felt when she had seen his reaction to her. Achingly she fought against recalling the subtle timbre in Mitch's voice when he'd told her, 'A man finds it erotic when a woman watches him making love to her, when she admires his body and takes pleasure in the effect she has on it...'

Her skin broke out in a rash of goose-bumps despite the steamy heat of the bathroom; her breasts felt heavy and tender, her thighs oddly weak. She ached inside, and if she closed her eyes...

Abruptly she moved, awkwardly snatching up her clean underwear as she tried to deny what was happening to her, brought close to the edge of tears by her inability to understand why she was reacting like this. Was it something to do with her age...her single state...was it some odd manifestation of the ticking away of her biological time-clock...or was it something that was caused by the trauma of her aunt's illness, a way of trying to side-track herself away from the anguish of what was happening? Tiredly she shook her head, trying to dispel all thoughts of Mitch, including the very, very betraying ones which were causing her to wonder where he was this evening and with whom. A dinner with a business colleague, he had said, and she wondered if that colleague was male or female. And if female...

Thoroughly alarmed by the direction of her thoughts, she brought them to an abrupt halt. It was her aunt she should be thinking of now, not Mitch Fletcher. *He* had no real place in her life, and he certainly had no place in her thoughts...or in her emotions.

When she got to the hospice her aunt was conscious, and very distressed. Holding her hand, Georgia sat with her, soothing her, her heart aching with fear and love as she listened to her aunt talking about her childhood, mistaking her for her sister, who had been her own grandmother, but had not lived long enough to know her.

The hours ticked by, long, exhausting hours when her aunt sometimes surfaced from the past to the

present and was once again the loving caring adult
who had guided Georgia so caringly through the
trauma of her own childhood loss, who had given
her so much, who now needed her so much, Georgia
acknowledged as they talked, or rather as her aunt
talked and she listened.

For the first time now she heard about the young
man her aunt had hoped to marry and who had
been killed so tragically by war.

'We were lovers before he went, and I prayed afterwards that I had conceived his child.'

Georgia squeezed her hand comfortingly.

'I wanted that so much. I had lost him, but to
have borne his child. There is no pain like that of
wanting your lover's child, the physical evidence of
your love, and knowing that it can never, ever be.
One day, when you fall in love, you will know what
I mean, Georgia.'

She was growing tired, exhausted by the effort
of talking, pain etched deep into the lines of her
face as she focused on Georgia's face.

'The worst thing about all of this is knowing I'll
be leaving you on your own,' she told Georgia
softly.

Georgia shook her head, trying to conceal her
own tears.

'I won't be on my own. I'll always have your
love. You've given me so much...'

'No more than you've given me. When your
parents were killed and I had to step in...you
brought purpose to my life, Georgia, and not just
purpose, but love as well.'

She paused and then added quietly, 'If all this is too much for you, I...'

Fiercely Georgia shook her head.

'No, I want to be with you...to share it with you.'

Tiredly her aunt smiled at her, promising her softly, 'I don't think it will be too long now. Strange, I've always thought when the time came that I'd be so afraid, that I'd have to pretend that I wasn't...but I'm not. I feel extraordinarily at peace.' She closed her eyes, causing Georgia's heart to pound with sick terror as she fought her desire to cry out, No...not yet. And then suddenly she opened them again as though she had heard that silent cry, and added faintly, 'It won't be yet. Not now, tonight, but soon...'

While she slept Georgia sat with her, afraid to move, tears pouring down her face, so that when Sister found her she remonstrated gently with her, telling her firmly, 'You must go home and rest, Georgia, otherwise when your aunt needs you most you'll be too exhausted to be with her. You've been here all night.'

All night! Dazedly Georgia looked towards the window, shocked to see that outside it was almost daylight.

'Go home,' Sister repeated, and then, correctly reading her mind, she added, 'It's all right. If for any reason your aunt needs you we'll get in touch with you. She's resting quietly now and the pain is under control.'

Georgia swallowed, and begged, 'How long?'

Sister shook her head. 'Not very long; two days...maybe three. We learn to recognise here when death is imminent...when our patients are ready to accept it. Now be a good girl and go home and rest. I promise you that your aunt will still be here with us when you come back.'

Realising that the sister meant what she said, Georgia got tiredly to her feet. She was exhausted, drained emotionally and mentally as well as physically. The night had taken an exacting toll on her. She gave a small shudder as she forced herself to walk away from her aunt's bed, unable to stop herself turning to look at her before she finally left the ward.

Her aunt would still be here when she returned, Sister had said, and implicit in those words had been the reassurance that she would still be alive...

Even so...even as she drove home in the clear light of the dawning summer day, Georgia promised herself that she would stay within earshot of the telephone.

Rest, Sister had commanded her, and yet how on earth was that going to be possible? Halfway home she almost turned the car round and drove back to the hospice, the only thing stopping her being the knowledge that Sister would send her right back again.

The hospice, under pressure to make full use of its available space for the people who needed it most, had few facilities for relatives of its patients who wanted to stay. She was lucky: she was within easy travelling distance of the hospice. And she knew herself how desperately her body physically needed sleep and how impossible it was for her to get the rest she needed propped up in a chair beside her aunt's bed; and yet she wanted to be with her...would be with her when the time finally came.

Her hands clenched on the steering-wheel, the road blurring in front of her. She lifted one hand to her face, fiercely brushing away the tears threatening to blind her.

It was an unpleasant shock when she got home to discover Mitch's car was parked outside. As she walked exhaustedly down the path towards the back door, she reminded herself that he had said something about having it serviced, and prayed hopefully that it had been returned after he had gone to work and that its presence outside the cottage didn't mean that Mitch himself was inside it.

She unlocked the back door. The kitchen was immaculate, and for a moment she thought that her prayer had been answered and that Mitch was out; and then she saw the jug of filter coffee and heard footsteps on the stairs, her body tensing as Mitch walked into the kitchen.

'So you're back, then.'

His voice was flat, devoid of any nuance of emotion, so why did she have the feeling that he was holding back an intense surge of anger? 'Do you often make a habit of staying out all night?' he pressed, his voice less metallic, roughening as he gave way to the rage she had sensed in him. 'Only I should like to know. Just so that I don't make a fool of myself by alerting the local police to the fact that you've disappeared. I'm not talking about a minute-by-minute, blow-by-blow description of how you've spent your time,' he went on sarcastically. 'Far from it. Just a few words of explanation... a brief note...'

Georgia still hadn't spoken. The unexpectedness of his attack on her had left her too stunned to defend herself. He was, she recognised with exhausted disbelief, behaving like an irate parent chastising a rebellious, difficult teenager.

She shook off the lethargic feeling of pain and despair that was her legacy of the night's events, trying to clear her head, her thoughts... to summon her defences.

'I'm not answerable to you,' she told him fiercely. 'This is my home, and I'm an adult. If I want to stay out all night, then that's my affair and no one else's.'

'*Affair* being exactly the right choice of word,' he cut in brutally, 'but you're wrong, you know. I'm sure your lover's wife would think it very much her business, as well as yours. Where was she, by the way? Safely out of the way somewhere, no doubt. Where did he take you? Some sordid, grubby little hotel, or did he take you home with him and make love to you in the bed he shares with his wife? Doing that turns some men on... and some women...'

The disgust in his voice made Georgia's skin crawl. Did he really think... was he actually suggesting...?

'Whatever happened between the pair of you last night, it's obvious that he couldn't wait to get rid of you this morning. Hardly a romantic lover... but then married men seldom are. They can't afford to be.'

Georgia had heard enough. His totally unfounded accusations coming on top of the trauma of the night sent her self-control crashing to the ground, her emotions spilling through her in wild turmoil so that she cried out bitterly.

'What do you know about it? What do you know about anything? What gives you the right to sit in judgement on me...to condemn me?'

To her horror she felt tears stinging her eyes, and knew that if she didn't get herself back under control she would break down completely. This was the last thing she could handle right now. She needed peace, solitude, sleep... She was, she discovered, trembling almost violently, her nerves so on edge, so jarred, her body so tense and so taut, that it would take only the least little thing to send her right over the edge. She wanted, she discovered in terror, to open her mouth and scream at him and to go on screaming until there was nothing left...no pain, no anger, no bitterness, no anguish...nothing.

'Was it really worth it?' she heard Mitch demand bitingly. 'Did you really honestly enjoy it, knowing that he was deceiving someone else to be with you, that he was cheating on a woman he had once purported to love, just as he'll cheat on you one day? You're an intelligent woman. Can you really not look beyond the present and see what lies in the future...don't you realise...?'

Georgia had had enough.

'I realise that you have no right to speak to me like this,' she told him thickly.

She felt almost punch-drunk, her mind woolly, her thought processes so slowed down and clogged up that it was almost physically impossible to think logically. 'And for your information...' She broke off, her voice completely suspended with emotion as she thought of how she had spent the night—the night he had accused her of spending in the arms of her supposed lover, in the bed he shared with his wife—knowing that there was no way she could tell him the truth.

A wave of sickness dizzied her, so that she had to put her hand on to the worktop to support herself. All she wanted to do was to be on her own, to try and get some much-needed rest so that when the crisis came, when the final hours of her aunt's life came, she would have the strength to support her through them.

'What are you doing here anyway?' she demanded groggily. 'I thought you'd have left for work by now.'

She only realised the conclusions he was drawing from her words when she saw the way his face tightened as he agreed coldly, 'Yes, I'm sure you did. It never occurred to you, I suppose, that I might be concerned for you, that when I came in and realised that your car was missing...that *you* were missing...'

Georgia stared at him in disbelief. Was he trying to tell her that he had delayed his departure this morning out of concern for her? That was ridiculous...impossible.

'I don't believe you,' she told him firmly, reacting instinctively to what he had said.

'No, I don't suppose you do,' he agreed acidly. 'But nevertheless it happens to be true. However, now that you *are* back...' He shot back the sleeve of his jacket and glanced briefly at his watch. For some reason that small, very masculine action made her stomach lurch and her whole body go weak. Dimly she was aware of him saying something about having to spend a couple of days in London and not returning until later in the week, but she was so desperately anxious to be on her own that it was only later, when he had gone, that she realised what he had actually said.

As soon as she was sure that he had gone, she went shakily upstairs, grimacing in disgust as she saw her reflection in her bedroom mirror.

She looked awful, her eye make-up streaked and smeared from her tears, her face pale and puffy, her hair tousled and untidy, her clothes as creased as though she had slept in them. No wonder he had thought...

She started to shiver, goose-bumps breaking out on her arms, so that she hugged them around her body, trying to conserve her body heat.

Why had he attacked her like that, with such verbal ferocity that she had felt his scorn like so many physical blows? She had never been exposed to anyone's contempt before, had never imagined that she might be. He was so judgemental, so contemptuous...so...so bitter...and yet despite what he thought of her he had still been concerned enough to wait until she came home...to assure himself that she was safe.

She sat down on her bed, her mind filled with odd unconnected thoughts. He had been concerned for her ... despite everything he thought about her, he had been worried. He had cared ...

A huge lump rose in her throat. Not because of him, she assured herself quickly; no, her emotional see-sawing was not caused by any reaction to Mitchell Fletcher, it was purely and simply the result of her concern for her aunt. That was what was making her so vulnerable, so ... so weakeningly susceptible to the thoughts and feelings of others ... of him. He was wrong about her, but he had no way of knowing that ... the things he had said to her had been cruel and unkind as well as unjustified, and yet even as he'd said them she had had the feeling that his real anger, his real contempt had been reserved not so much for her, but for her partner, her supposed lover.

What was happening to her? she asked herself tiredly. *Why* was she allowing herself to see his point of view, to react so sympathetically, so dangerously to him? She had been angry enough at the time, furiously so ... and, had she not felt so physically weak, she could almost have retaliated by hitting out at him. She gave a small shudder of shocked recognition at how dangerously volatile her emotions had become.

Forget him, she instructed herself as she undressed. Forget him. You've got far more important things to worry about ... far, far more important.

CHAPTER SIX

FOR two days or so, it seemed to Georgia that her aunt miraculously rallied and seemed almost to be making a recovery; and then, on the third day, when Georgia had left her bedside to go home for a much-needed rest, the telephone rang, bringing her out of her deep and exhausted sleep.

She knew instinctively even before she answered it that it would be the hospice. Within ten minutes of the call she was dressed and on her way to her aunt's beside, trying to remind herself that it would serve no purpose if through lack of concentration on her driving she should suffer some form of accident on her way there.

Grimly she reflected that if Mitchell Fletcher should return in her absence he would no doubt once again think she was spending the night with her lover.

Mitchell Fletcher—what on earth was she doing letting him into her mind, her thoughts, her emotions now when she needed all her energies, all her emotional and mental resources to be concentrated on her aunt and what lay ahead?

Was it because she was so desperately afraid, even now, of letting her aunt down, of draining from her the last of her fragile strength, instead of giving to her, supporting her, that she allowed herself to think of Mitchell? Was she using him as a means of distracting herself from what lay ahead?

As she got closer to the hospice her stomach started to churn. Death as a concept was hard enough to face; but as a reality... She gave a tense shudder. She was so desperately afraid, she acknowledged, afraid both of letting her aunt down, and for herself. She had never witnessed death before, and the thought of witnessing her beloved aunt's...

It was a relief when she got to the hospice to find that her aunt was both conscious and lucid, even if she did look heartbreakingly frail.

'If you want one of us to sit with you, or if you need us at all...' Sister told her gently as she accompanied her to her aunt's bedside.

Silently Georgia shook her head, settling herself at her aunt's side, reaching for the impossibly frail, almost fleshless hand that lay outside the covers.

Amazingly, her aunt was actually smiling, her eyes so full of love and reassurance that, despite her determination not to do so, Georgia felt her own eyes fill with tears. Tears for herself, she told herself firmly, not for her aunt, who was so calm, so obviously at peace with herself that to cry for her would almost have been an insult to her bravery... an attempt to take from her what she had fought so hard to achieve.

'No, Georgia, don't,' her aunt chided her softly when she tried to hide her tears from her. 'There's no need to hide your feelings from me. I feel like crying a little myself. There's still so much I wanted to do... those roses, for instance. I wanted to see you married...to hold your children; and yet at the same time I feel...I feel a great sense of rejoicing...of calm and peace.' The fragile fingers tightened in Georgia's own. 'I'm not afraid of death, Georgia, although I admit there have been many, many times when I've feared the actual manner of my dying, and yet now I don't. There's no pain, no fear...'

Georgia swallowed hard, knowing from what she had been told that her aunt had been given sufficient drugs to ease her physical pain and yet at the same time to allow her to remain conscious, although the sister had warned Georgia that towards the end her aunt would lapse in and out of consciousness, and might on occasions either not recognise her, or confuse her with someone else.

'It isn't uncommon for someone close to death to imagine that they can see someone who's been very close to them and who has perhaps been dead for a long time, so don't be alarmed if that should happen with your aunt,' Sister had warned her.

Her aunt wanted to talk, and even though Georgia wanted to cry out to her not to do so, to preserve her strength, she managed to hold back the words, telling herself that it was her aunt's needs that must be paramount now and not her own. Sometimes, as Georgia had been warned would happen, she drifted in and out of consciousness, sometimes confusing Georgia with her sister, and sometimes with Georgia's own mother, but slowly, inexorably, her life-force was ebbing away, the fingers held within her own frighteningly cool to the touch, only the brilliance in her blue eyes when she turned them in Georgia's direction showing that life still burned within her.

Once she broke free of the gathering shadows, like a child fleeing from the dark, her voice unexpectedly strong as she begged, 'Hold on to me, Georgia . . . I'm so afraid . . .'

And then, almost immediately, as Georgia suppressed her own anguish to reach out and hold her tightly in her arms, an expression of intense peace illuminated her whole face.

Eerily, or so it seemed to Georgia, she appeared to be looking beyond her, focusing on something or someone that she herself could not see.

The ward was in darkness. The afternoon had long ago slid into the evening and the evening into night.

Almost as though she had known what was happening, Sister appeared beside the bed, moving on silent capable feet, to rest her hand on Georgia's shoulder, giving her warmth and strength, taking from her the icy cold that seemed to have engulfed her.

Georgia found she could hardly breathe, could hardly swallow, so great was her tension, her anguish. She heard her aunt say something . . . a name perhaps . . . a look of such rapturous shining joy softening her face that Georgia instinctively turned her head to look in the same direction, only she could see nothing other than the darkness surrounding the bed.

In the heavy silence of the ward, the sound from her aunt's throat as she drew her last breath sounded preternaturally loud.

Even before Sister's hand tightened on her shoulder, Georgia knew that she had gone, but she still continued to hold her, bending her head over her aunt's, as she gave way to the tears she had fought so long to suppress.

Understandingly Sister let her give way to her grief, before gently easing her away and even more gently laying her aunt's lifeless body back in the bed.

'Can I . . . is it all right if I stay here with her for a while?' Georgia whispered.

Quietly Sister nodded, moving away as silently as she had come.

Later Georgia had no knowledge of how long she had stayed there, sitting beside her aunt, nor could she remember what she had said to her, only that she had talked so much that later her throat had ached from it, or from her tears . . . She only knew that when Sister finally told her that it was time for her to leave she felt totally numb inside and out, aware of the fact that her aunt had died and yet still somehow unable to take it all in.

There would be arrangements to make . . . things to do . . . she knew that, and yet as she left the hospice to drive home she couldn't focus on them, couldn't focus on anything other than the disbelief that it was all over, that her aunt was actually dead.

When she got home she went straight to bed, needing the escape that sleep would provide.

She slept all day, woken early in the evening by the sun shining through her window.

It took several seconds for her to remember what had happened. When she did, she started to tremble violently, sick inside with shock and loss.

The phone rang, but she ignored it. She wasn't ready to face the world yet, to accept that her aunt's life was over. She wanted to be alone with her memories ... her grief ...

She got up, showered and washed her hair and then discovered that she felt too exhausted to bother getting dressed. Instead, she pulled on a towelling robe. Her aunt had bought it for her the previous Christmas, and as her fingers smoothed the softness of the towelling she could feel the tears welling up inside her. Quickly she closed her eyes, squeezing them together to suppress the tears. As she opened the bathroom door, she was standing opposite the door to her aunt's room.

Unsteadily she walked towards it and opened it. The scent of her aunt's lavender cologne still hung on the air. Her silver-backed hair brushes and mirror gleamed on the walnut dressing-table.

The set had been given to her on her twenty-first birthday by her parents. Slowly Georgia walked across the floor and picked up the mirror. Her aunt's date of birth and initials were inscribed on it. She touched the inscription with one finger. There was a hot burning sensation around her heart, an ache that just being here among her aunt's possessions seemed to ease, as though the room itself possessed a cooling, soothing balm. She looked at the bed, remembering how often as a child, in the early months after her parents' death, she had gone running into her aunt's room, to be picked up and lifted on to her bed to be cuddled and loved.

Had she ever told her aunt how much she loved her ... how much she appreciated all she had done for her? Had she ever shown her, as she herself had been shown, how strong her love was...?

Feelings of guilt and despair filled her. She had a desperate need to turn back the clock, to tell her aunt all the things she feared she had left unsaid. She could feel herself starting to shake as her own guilt reproached her for a thousand now sharply remembered small misdemeanours. Shakily she walked towards the door, closing it behind her before going into her own room. Her eyes were blurred with tears. She sat down on her bed, reaching out for her handbag, searching for her handkerchief, but she was trembling so much that she knocked the bag over, its contents disgorging themselves on to the bed and the floor. Her aunt's keys lay on the bed beside her, and the sight of them, bringing home to her the reality of her aunt's death, made her cry out in anguish and denial, her grief overwhelming her as she stared at them, protesting achingly, 'No...no...no...'

Engrossed in her grief, she didn't hear the car outside, nor the door being unlocked, and it wasn't until she heard Mitch demanding urgently from the open doorway, 'What is it—what's wrong?' that she realised he was even in the house.

She turned automatically at the sound of his voice, too startled to think of trying to conceal her grief, oblivious to the fact that her towelling robe was clinging damply to her obviously bare body, and not aware of the conclusion he was drawing from her distraught state. Even when he said roughly, 'It's over, isn't it?' she confusedly believed that he was referring to her aunt's death, too upset to do anything more than nod her head in acknowledgement as he stepped into the room, noting her upturned handbag, and the spare set of keys to the house.

'I tried to warn you that this would happen,' she heard him saying, the words bouncing off her, having no meaning to her, her grief-stricken face turning in his direction as she tried to focus on him.

'Oh, God, how could he do this to you?' she heard him saying, and then he was sitting on the bed beside her, reaching out to her, offering her the comfort of his arms, his warmth...offering her the physical compassion she so desperately needed, the sensation of being held close to him so reminiscent of the love she had received from her aunt that she accepted it blindly, letting him hold her while she gave way to her grief, barely aware of who he was, only that he offered her comfort as she clung to him.

When she felt him brushing the damp hair back off her face and trying to ease some physical distance between them, she reacted instinctively, resisting his attempts to move back from her, clinging on to him, protesting thickly, 'No...please...'

He felt so safe, so warm...the scent of his skin was so comforting, so...so compelling. She wanted to stay like this, held in his arms for ever. She trembled, her emotions, her needs veering so sharply from those of a child to those of a woman that she herself was barely aware of what had happened, only of the intense need to stay with him, to draw from him a surcease to the complex desires that drove her.

When his hand touched her shoulder, attempting to move her gently away from him, she clung on to him, the damp towelling fabric slipping free of her body, revealing the satin-smooth curve of her throat and shoulder, the rounded softness of her arm and the full curve of her breast.

'Georgia...'

Her mind, her senses registered the protest, the denial in his voice, but something deeper, something instinctive and feminine, recognised that beyond that denial lay a masculine desire, a masculine responsiveness to her femininity. Frantically she reached out towards it, wanting it, needing it, her mind yielding totally to the demands of her body, her emotions.

She reached out for the hand he had lifted from her body, her fingers on his wrist, her unexpected show of strength taking him off guard so that she was leaning towards him, and urging his hand towards her breast before he could stop her, her lips soft and parted as she whispered against his mouth, 'Please...please...I need you...'

She heard him gasp, felt his hesitation and might have reacted to it, might have allowed reality to come crashing through the torment of her grief and realised what she was doing, if her chilled skin hadn't suddenly reacted to the cool air and the touch of his hand, her nipple hardening, pushing against his touch, causing him to respond instinctively to its allure, the rough pad of his thumb immediately circling the hard nub of flesh, his mouth unexpectedly, fiercely almost, opening over hers, taking

the initiative from her, leaving her drowning in a
tide of sensation she had no strength to resist.

Both his hands were on her breasts now, caressing her body in a way totally outside her experience, making her ache and yearn, making her
forget everything but the desire that was burning
out of control inside her.

She had never experienced anything like it in her
life, never dreamed there could be such wanting,
such intensity, such sharp-edged and compulsive
desire. It overwhelmed her, completely obliterating
everything else, making her moan achingly beneath
the pressure of Mitch's kiss. She shrugged herself
out of her robe, her senses responding fiercely to
the deep tremor of reaction that ran through him
as she pressed herself against him, running her
hands along his shoulders and down over his back,
feeling the muscles beneath his skin tense as she
touched him, knowing with some deep atavistic
feminine awareness that he wanted her, and shockingly glorying in that knowledge, glorying in the
power of her body, her femininity to arouse him.
She arched herself against him as his hands touched
her body, cupping her breasts . . . stroking over her
ribcage, her waist, her hips, following the rounded
curve of her bottom as he pulled her against him,
holding her so close that she could feel the hard
pressure of his erection.

It seemed not to matter that she had never done
anything like this before, that she had never imagined, nor even wanted to imagine herself being
so totally lost to restraint, to self-control, to her
deeply rooted belief that such sexual intensity be-

longed only to an equal intensity of emotional love.
She wanted this man . . . needed him . . . ached for
him . . .

She told him as much, whispering the words between small sobbed moans of pleasure, breathing
them shakily into his ear when he responded to her
whispered pleas, telling him how much she was enjoying the rough abrasion of his fingertips against
her skin, how much she needed the heat of his
mouth, the delicate stroke of his tongue, the
strength and power of his body, saying things to
him that she had never dreamed she knew how to
say, communicating to him the depth and intensity
of her need with a sensuality she had never known
she possessed.

It was almost as though another person had taken
control of her . . . as though she had undergone a
powerful, irresistible change of personality.

She tugged impatiently at his shirt, wanting the
freedom to touch him as he was doing her, almost
sobbing with impatience as she struggled with the
small buttons, and then brought equally close to
tears of relief when he helped her with them, his
hands trembling a little as he tugged the shirt off
and then started to unfasten his belt.

She watched him dry-mouthed, her heart
pounding, her senses so caught up in the full tide
of her own desire that there was no room within
her for anything else. Her breathing quickened as
he stepped out of his clothes.

Once before she had seen him like this . . . Then
she had not allowed herself to recognise her response to his masculinity. Then she had fought off

her awareness of him as a man and the effect his maleness was having on her. This time...

She knelt on the bed, oblivious to her own nakedness, watching him, her eyes huge and round, the irises dark with arousal. As she studied him her body trembled, her tongue-tip moistening her dry lips. She heard him say something, the words unimportant, the raw, needing tone of his voice saying all that needed to be said, sending a quiver of response running through her, coiling the muscles of her stomach, swelling her breasts.

'Do you know what you do to me when you look at me like that?' she heard Mitch groan as he reached for her. 'You make me feel as though I'm the only man you've ever seen, the only man you ever want to see. You look at me as though you can't see enough of my body. You make me feel as though you'd die to touch me... to love me...'

His voice had dropped to a harsh whisper. She could see the strain in his eyes, the desire, the need. Even if his body hadn't already proclaimed its desire for her, his voice, his eyes, the way he trembled slightly as he held her would have told her just as surely.

'Touch me, Georgia,' she heard him begging her. 'Touch me... kiss me... love me... because if you don't... I'm going to...' He broke off and then cursed. 'Oh, God, I can't...' His voice was muffled, strained, and then his mouth was on her breast, gently at first as though he was half afraid of hurting her, and then, as his control deserted him, less gently, so that she cried out in fierce pleasure, arching against him, inviting his passion, igniting it with the abandonment of her body to him.

When he touched her intimately she moved eagerly against him, holding his hand against her body when he would have moved away, telling him how much pleasure he was giving her, pleading with him not to stop what he was doing, but this time he resisted her, easing her away from him, saying something she didn't hear until he repeated it, his voice harsh and almost angry as he told her.

'I can't, Georgia. I can't make love to you. I don't have any way of protecting you . . . and, God help me, I can't trust myself not to . . .'

It took seconds for her to understand what he was trying to tell her, and when he did her body registered her resentment, its denial of the caution he was trying to instil in her.

He was starting to move away from her, but the sight of his body, so male, so aroused, so perfectly designed to satisfy her every sensual need, made her reach out towards him, digging her fingers into his wrist as she fought to stop him leaving her.

'Mitch . . . No, please . . . I want you.'

She heard herself crying out the words, and registered their abandonment, their wantonness with a tiny shocked corner of her mind that could not conceive that this was actually her, Georgia, saying these things, behaving like this.

'Shush . . . shush . . . it's all right, it's all right.'

Mitch was holding her again, not close to his body as she ached to be held, but at least he was holding her. His hand cupped her breast. She heard him catch his breath as she moved urgently against him. He had slid down over her body and between her legs. Tiny shudders of tension rippled through her as he touched her. She closed her eyes, her nails digging into his shoulder as she clung on to him. When he pushed her down on the bed, she trembled with need and anticipation, keeping her eyes tightly closed as she prayed that this time he wouldn't move away from her, gasping with shocked pleasure as she felt his mouth caressing her waist, her stomach, and then lower, his hand easing her thighs apart as his mouth caressed their silky inner flesh.

She cried out in protest, not ready to accept this level of intimacy, but he had already anticipated her tension, soothing her body with his hands as he whispered against her skin.

'Shush, it's all right. I only want to please you, Georgia. To show you...' He stopped speaking, biting gently on her flesh, making her forget her denial of him as her body responded helplessly to his sensuality, making her cry out pleadingly to him when he caressed her with tender intimacy. The touch of his hands and mouth was so caring and sure that she had no way of controlling the intensity of her response to him, helplessly giving in to the sharply violent shudders of pleasure that contracted her muscles, crying out to him in the shock and wonder of it, and then later crying in his arms as he held her and soothed her, stroking her skin, comforting her overwrought senses, holding her while she fell into an exhausted sleep in his arms, bitterly envying her lover, the man he knew all the passion had really been meant for...the man who had rejected her to no doubt go back to his wife.

Dear God, if *he* had been her lover... if *he* had been the one... His arms tightened around her sleeping body. He had known almost from the first moment he met her how he felt about her. Had known it and had tried to ignore it. He had always been so wary, so careful not to allow himself to fall in love... not to allow himself to want any woman to this extent, knowing that for him the commitment he would want to give and would need to demand in return would mean marriage... a marriage that would have to last a lifetime. And now he had gone and broken all his own rules: he had fallen in love with a woman who it was obvious loved someone else... a woman who had used him sexually as a stand-in for the man she really wanted. He shuddered, knowing that for his pride's sake he ought to leave now, and knowing equally that he was physically incapable of doing so.

She moved in his arms, unexpectedly opening her eyes, her own blurred with sleep, shadowed and dark. She reached for him, opening her arms to him, looking straight into his eyes as she begged softly, 'Make love to me, Mitch. I need you to so much. I don't care that you can't... that you don't... It doesn't matter anyway.'

As she heard herself speak the words, Georgia felt a tiny tremor start somewhere deep inside her, a small crack in the protective bubble that had surrounded her ever since the moment of her aunt's death, and briefly she surfaced to face reality, the shock of what she was doing tensing her body...but then Mitch was touching her, protesting to her that she was too much temptation for him, holding her, guiding her hands to his body as he begged her to love him as he had loved her, moving so powerfully against her when she did touch him that the awe of his body's response to her swept everything else away.

She had wanted to know him with this intimacy, she acknowledged as she touched him and felt her own body's response to his arousal. She had wanted to caress him with her hands and her mouth... had wanted to explore his masculinity, to know him as intimately as it was possible for a woman to know a man.

Driven on by her senses, by needs which had been born as her aunt died, needs which drowned out all the warning cautionary shocked voice of reason and reality which would have tried to make her realise just what she was doing, she stroked and kissed him, slowly caressing each part of his body, luxuriating in her freedom to do so. She knew, each time he shuddered and protested thickly against what she was doing, that deep within her own body there was an answering response, an answering need; that, even while she was enjoying the pleasure of touching him, she was also enjoying the knowledge that she was deliberately inciting him to the point where he would take hold of her and love her, possess her, his body moving powerfully within her, quickening her flesh with responsive desire. And even then, knowing that, she was still unaware of what really drove her, of her own instinctive need to create life in the place of death... Why should she know that, despite all the antagonism there had been between them, there would be this passion, this needing...this aching compulsive wanting that neither of them seemed able to contain, as he finally gave in to her whispered pleas and demands and she felt the heat and strength of him moving inside her, filling her; flooding her first with desire and need, and then later with such intense satisfaction that her body could hardly endure to let him go?

This time, when she slept, Mitch forced himself to leave her, sick at heart, with himself and with her. Her pleasure, her whispered words of love, her rapturous response to his lovemaking, her shining tears of fulfilment—none of them had been meant for him, no matter how much she had made him feel as though he was the one man...the only man who could give her such pleasure, such satisfaction.

He acquitted her of wanting him through any depraved need to punish her ex-lover, or satisfy some gross sexual desire. She had been too far beyond that kind of calculation...lost, or so it seemed, in another world...the look in her eyes sometimes so far away and unfocused that he had even wondered if she knew just who she was with, if within her heart and her mind she had actually substituted him for her lover. He had wanted to shake her then, to tell her who he was, to make her say his name, make her realise...But how could he blame her when he himself had been unable to resist, unable to control...unable to stop himself giving in to his need for her, his love for her? He couldn't continue to stay here now, not after what had happened; and she, he suspected, would not want him to. When she woke up in the morning, the last face she would want to see would be his. And if he did stay... He shuddered deeply. How long would it be before he lost all sense of pride, of maleness, before he started begging her to give him the emotional commitment he craved?

He loved her, he recognised broodingly as he slid out of the bed, taking care not to disturb her, standing beside her as he looked down at her sleeping figure, aching to take hold of her and tell her how he felt... to beg her to forget the other man, a man who had made it plain that he wasn't worthy of her. But he suppressed the urge, knowing his love wasn't what she wanted. Knowing that *he* wasn't who she wanted.

Silently he collected his things, moving soft-footed through the dark house, careful not to disturb her deep sleep, as he finally gathered together the last of his things and, unable to resist one last look at her, returned to the bedroom and her sleeping figure.

Unable to stop himself, he bent over her, kissing her forehead, and then her mouth, touching the tender flesh of her arm, shuddering deeply as the moonlight revealed the soft curve of her breast.

His memories of this night would remain with him for the rest of his life. He doubted if she would remember him for as long as next week, unless it was with anger and resentment. His mouth compressing, he walked towards the open door.

In her sleep, Georgia stirred, making a soft sound of protest, her forehead creasing in a frown, her sleep momentarily disturbed by fear and dread, by the heavy weight of emotional loss and pain; but then sleep claimed her again and she sank back gratefully on to it, needing its oblivion.

Outside Mitch took one last look at the cottage before getting in his car and driving away.

On the kitchen table was the note he had left behind him explaining that he had business in London, and that he thought it best from both their points of view if he terminated their arrangements.

The money he had paid over to her in rent was not to be repaid, he had written, and he wished her well for the future. He left no forwarding address.

CHAPTER SEVEN

GEORGIA didn't want to wake up; she was too conscious of the black pit of misery that lay waiting for her once she let awareness slide in beneath the comforting blanket of sleep. And yet already it was too late.

Already she was conscious of the morning sounds of the birds beyond her window, of the sunlight streaming into the room, both of which seemed cruelly out of tune with her emotions.

No birds should be singing. No sun should be shining. Instead the day should be mirroring her mood, the sky dark and leaden, too grey and heavy for the relief even of rain.

Her aunt was dead; only now was her mind truly accepting that reality. She gave a deep shudder as mental images flickered painfully behind her shuttered eyelids: her aunt lying in her hospice bed, holding her, talking to her, losing consciousness and then, just before the end, rallying briefly. She squeezed her eyes tightly closed and then tensed abruptly as other different images imposed themselves on her memory... images which had nothing to do with the long hours she had spent at her aunt's bedside, images which surely could be nothing but pure fantasy...images which could not be real, and yet which her senses were telling her were real.

She sat up in bed, stifling a shocked gasp as she realised she was naked. As she moved too abruptly, her muscles tensed again, her body aching slightly. Her towelling robe lay neatly folded on a chair by the window, and momentarily the sight of it was reassuringly normal—its very neatness denied that it could ever have been discarded with the passionate abandonment her senses seemed to suggest, but then, as she turned her head and looked towards her closed bedroom door, she saw the dent in the pillow next to her own, and when she reached out to touch it, her fingers trembling, her touch against the crumpled linen released a faint and very masculine scent of soap and cologne which she recognised instantly.

Was it true, then? Had she and Mitchell Fletcher been lovers last night? Had she clung to him, pleading and begging for his touch, his kiss...his body...?

She made an appalled sound of denial deep in her throat, a tiny half-animal moan of rejection of a knowledge that her mind would not allow her.

Relentlessly ignoring her desperate plea to stop, her memory recalled for her snatched words, senses...touches from the night, each one more appalling, more self-condemning than the last.

As she writhed in anguish, clenching her muscles against what her mind was telling her, the realisation of what she had done refused to go away.

And she could not blame him...could not pretend even to herself that it had been his fault, his instigation, or even his desire that had led to their being lovers. No, *she* had been the one who...

Georgia shuddered sickly, recalling with unwanted clarity the things she had said to him, the pleas she had made...the way she had touched him; and even as she did so she could hardly comprehend that she had actually behaved in such a way. It seemed so alien, so...so unbelievable. It couldn't be true. And yet she knew that it was.

What had happened to her? Why had she behaved in a way that was totally out of character for her? She cringed, remembering against her will the pleasure he had given her, the intensity of her own desire, the ache to touch him, to...to love him. But why...why? She hardly knew him...didn't even like him...and yet she had been sexually responsive to him in a way she had never even dreamed she was capable of being.

A shudder of disgust went through her as she castigated herself for her lack of self-control. To have behaved like that, so soon after witnessing her aunt's death... Sickness clawed at her stomach. She pushed back the bedclothes and ran to the bathroom.

Ten minutes later, staring in the mirror at her ashen-faced dishevelment, she suppressed a harsh sound of self-disgust. She turned on the shower and stood under it while its icy spray scoured her body, as though somehow she could wash away her memories of what she had done.

No, she couldn't blame Mitchell Fletcher for what had happened, she told herself grimly when she was dressed. He had simply taken what she had offered...and why not? Men were like that, weren't they? At least some of them were...although...

She frowned, chewing on her bottom lip. Had she been asked to judge, she would have guessed that Mitch Fletcher was not the kind of man who would ever succumb easily to any physical appetite. She had thought him more self-controlled, more...more discerning, and he had made it plain enough just how he viewed her...and her supposed relationship with her married lover.

A bitter smile curled her mouth. She had only had one lover. She closed her eyes, swaying slightly as she recalled against her will how intensely, how passionately she had encouraged Mitch to make love to her...how despite her lack of experience, her lack of practical knowledge, she had somehow known... He might have been her first lover but her body had wanted him, welcomed him with an eagerness, a knowingness that had made a mockery of the diffidence, the tension, the apprehension with which a woman was supposed to approach her first full sexual experience.

Thankfully she had the house to herself. She had looked out of the window and seen that Mitch's car was missing. She didn't know how on earth she was ever going to be able to face him. Last night had obviously been some kind of mental aberration, some kind of reaction to her aunt's death; that was the only rational explanation she could find for her otherwise inexplicable behaviour. But would he...would Mitch believe it? Would he even care what had motivated her? Would he...?

She frowned as she walked into the kitchen and saw the folded note propped up on the table.

Something warned her even before she opened it just what it was going to contain. She read it quickly, dropping it on to the table as though it burned, her face going white and then red as she recognised all that the brief, polite note did not say.

He was disgusted by her... sickened by her behaviour—and why not? She felt the same way herself. No wonder he had decided to leave, no wonder... She trembled, picking up the note again, absently smoothing out the paper. His handwriting was clear and well-formed. She discovered that she was staring at his signature, greedily absorbing it, her fingertip tracing it, as last night she had traced an erotic path along the inside of his thigh when... She swallowed hard, confused and appalled by what she was feeling. The last thing she wanted was to have to face him, to have to read in his eyes his awareness, his knowledge of what she had done; and yet instead of being relieved by the contents of his note she felt... she felt lost, abandoned, deserted and rejected, she recognised sickly. She felt, she admitted as she pulled out a chair and sat down on it, bereft, in much the same way as she had felt last night when her aunt died. She gave a small shudder. But that was idiotic, impossible... Mitch Fletcher meant nothing to her... less than nothing, in fact. She hardly knew him...

Against her will her mind corrected her, flashing tiny images of him across her brain, mercilessly reinforcing just how much she did know about him: the way he walked, for instance, the changing expression in his eyes, the way he moved... the scent of his body, the taste and feel of it.

Physical knowledge, she derided herself. It meant nothing.

But her knowledge of him was not just physical; it went much deeper than that. He was compassionate, caring. He held very strong and firm views on life. Ironically, views that were very much in line with her own. Like him, she believed that it was necessary for two people to work hard to keep a relationship healthy and alive...that, once a commitment to another person was given, it was given for life, not merely for as long as the sexual excitement between them lasted; and yet last night...

The phone rang, mercifully cutting across her painful examination, and yet when she reached for it, answering it and recognising the voice of the sister from the hospital, she felt a sharp pang of disappointment as though she had been hoping, wanting her caller to be someone else...as though her senses had been anticipating, longing for the sound of a male voice.

She was sorry to disturb her, Sister was saying, but there were formalities to be attended to, things to be done.

Shakily Georgia listened to her, grateful for her gentle advice and suggestions. The funeral would be very quiet, they knew so few people locally, and before that, in the busy suburb where she had grown up, people came and went, and her aunt had always been a very private sort of person.

The small town boasted an ancient church with a traditional graveyard and Georgia knew that it was here that her aunt wished to be buried.

*   *   *

The next few days passed in a pain-filled daze; there were things to be done, arrangements to be made, things to keep her busy and her thoughts occupied, and yet despite this the pain of her loss was a burden that was always there.

At night she couldn't sleep, lying open-eyed and physically exhausted in her bed, remembering things from her childhood, her growing and teenage years...remembering all the small and large sacrifices her aunt had made for her...remembering and aching to be able to tell her how much she appreciated all that she had done.

What had happened with Mitch was something she had pushed to the back of her mind, unable to cope both with that and her aunt's death.

People had been kind, compassionate and understanding, but the loss was hers and not theirs. She felt isolated from them, alone in a way that when she dwelt on it made her feel very, very afraid. It was as though there were an actual physical barrier between her and other people, as though her grief cut her off from them in some way, rendering her separate and apart.

She couldn't eat or sleep, and was constantly nauseous. Nothing around her seemed to have any reality.

These were all things commonly experienced following the death of a close relative or friend, Sister explained gently to her, urging kindly, 'It helps if you have someone to talk to. Too often after a death others draw back, afraid of mentioning the dead person...afraid of appearing lacking in sensitivity. But often what that person needs and wants the most is someone to talk to...someone to listen while they talk about the person they've lost.

'We do have a counselling service to help people through this period. If you would like me to...'

Immediately Georgia shook her head.

'No. No, I'll be all right,' she told her huskily. 'I have to get back to work...and there are so many things to do. My aunt's clothes...her papers... And then there are the roses...'

She was aware of the compassionate silence that greeted her quick, defensive denial of any need for help, but the last thing she wanted was to talk about her aunt to someone else...someone who had not known her...who didn't know...

She was behaving irrationally, Georgia recognised, and yet she was powerless to do anything about it. She felt as though every muscle, every fibre of her body were screwed up into a tense ball of rejection...as though she couldn't endure having anyone come close to her physically or emotionally.

Louise Mather had offered to help her with the arrangements for the funeral, but Georgia had refused that offer. This was the final service she could do for her aunt...the final proof of her love...the final test.

She was being governed, driven almost by emotions, needs she could not even begin to analyse, her fears, her guilt emphasised by the way she had behaved on the night of her aunt's death. Her memories of that night were something that continued to taunt and torment her. She could not forget or dismiss them no matter how hard she tried.

No wonder that Mitch had left the way he did. He must have been disgusted with her...but no more disgusted than she was herself. She found she could not stop thinking about him...could not stop remembering. Why was it that her memory, her imagination kept on conjuring up images of him touching her with not merely passion and desire but with tenderness, emotion, caring as well...things she knew it must have been impossible for him to feel, as though even her own mind had to cloak what she had done in the fallacy of some kind of emotional bonding between them...a bonding she was well aware could not possibly have existed.

She felt like someone caught in a trap, so that, no matter how hard she twisted and turned, she could not break free of it. It was as though, in joining herself to him physically, she had somehow or other created a need within herself for him emotionally as well. As though her physical intimacy with him had created within her a craving for him... Anyone would think that she loved him, not merely had sex with him, she told herself bitterly on the morning of her aunt's funeral. That was how she was behaving: like a woman in love, and not one who had merely given in to some grotesque sexual impulse!

The funeral was quiet, and yet somehow uplifting...soothing...leaving her with an odd awareness of the rightness of things, an unexpected sense of peace to soothe the sharp ache of her loss.

Despite her protests, Louise had insisted on accompanying her, standing just a few steps behind her at the graveside.

It was still a cool morning, without any breeze, and before coming out Georgia had cut every single blossom from the rose bushes, tying them with a simple piece of silk ribbon. As she laid them on the coffin her eyes blurred with tears, and the sharp, acrid taste of nausea filled her throat.

Just because she was no longer with Georgia in the physical sense, that did not mean that her love for her had gone, her aunt had told her before she died. That would always be there for her.

Despite the fact that it was the last thing Georgia wanted to do, Louise insisted on taking her home with her after the funeral, sitting her down at her kitchen table and virtually standing over her while she toyed with the meal she had prepared.

'I know how much your aunt meant to you,' Louise told her gently. 'But, Georgia, the last thing she would have wanted would be for you to neglect your own health. You're too thin already. Look, why don't you have a holiday? Go somewhere sunny and try to relax . . . to get over things?'

Georgia shook her head.

'No, not yet. Maybe later. Right now . . . I've got to keep busy, Louise,' she told her friend desperately. 'I have to find my own way of working through what I'm feeling. It's almost as though there's no purpose in my life any more...no reason to go on.' She saw Louise's face and shivered. 'I'm being over-dramatic, I know . . .'

'It's not that. I can understand how you feel. Your aunt has been the focus of your life ever since you came here, and of course with her gone you're bound to feel...'

'Alone?'

'It would probably be different if you had other family.'

'Maybe.'

'Oh, by the way, I meant to ask you, did Mitch Fletcher say anything about his reasons for returning to London so unexpectedly?'

Georgia tensed, shooting her friend a brief nervous glance.

'I'm not asking you to break any confidences,' Louise continued. 'It's just that I had heard he was thinking of transferring his head office operation down here, and naturally, if he does, that could mean more work for us. Conversely, if he's changed his mind and is perhaps thinking of closing the factory down here...'

'He didn't say anything to me about his business plans,' Georgia told her in a low voice.

For some reason she badly wanted to cry. The very sound of Mitch's name had provoked a churning sensation in her stomach coupled with a yearning emotional ache that left her stripped bare of the pretence she had been trying to impose on herself that he meant nothing to her, that what had happened had happened purely because of her aunt's death and had nothing whatsoever to do with Mitch Fletcher personally.

'I...I think I'd like to go home...'

She got up unsteadily, ignoring Louise's concerned protests that she did not think she ought to be alone. Solitude suddenly was something she craved, needing to come to terms with the significance of what she had just experienced.

Once she got home she went upstairs and opened the door to the bedroom Mitch had occupied. It looked neat and bare, empty of any memory of him. She went and sat down on the bed...his bed... She looked at the untouched white pillow. His head had once lain there. She closed her eyes, visualising it, feeling the now familiar stomach-clenching pain that attacked her, welcoming its punishment, embracing it almost, telling herself that it was what she deserved for feeling like this...fool that she was for falling so ridiculously in love with a man who had patently not wanted that love.

Fallen in love...her mouth twisted in a bitter smile. Why hadn't she realised the truth before...before it was too late...before she had deliberately and evasively hidden it from herself?

Yes, of course, the trauma of her aunt's death had released her inhibitions, destroyed her self-control, sent her, for a little while at least, almost out of her mind with shock and grief; but it hadn't just been that that had made her turn to Mitch, that had made her beg and plead with him to make love to her. Her body, her senses had known then what her mind had refused to recognise. Wasn't that, after all, why she had never attempted to tell him the truth, to correct his misconception of her, to explain to him that there was no married lover— because she had known that if she did, if she removed that barrier between them, she would be vulnerable to him and to her own feelings?

She covered her face with her hands, giving way to shock and grief.

Had she no pride, no self-respect? She knew he didn't love her. She had known it that night, but she had ignored that knowledge and instead...

She made a low, tortured sound of pain. No wonder he had left so quickly. Had he realised what she had tried to keep from herself, had he seen beyond her apparent antagonism and recognised her true feelings for him? She prayed not. She prayed that he had simply believed she was using him because her lover had deserted her.

She gave another tense shudder. She felt sick again... She got up, heading for the bathroom.

It was so exhausting, this constant sickness, and she had hardly eaten anything at all today, only the meal Louise had prepared for her.

It was her aunt's death, of course. People reacted in different ways to loss and grief, she knew that...not that she was normally the type of person who suffered constant attacks of nausea; in fact...

There were things she ought to be doing, but somehow she simply could not summon the energy. She felt drained, empty... exhausted and yet at the same time reluctant to do anything to rouse herself from her lethargy. It was a protective island beyond which the sharks of loneliness, pain and despair lay waiting to savage her with sharp teeth. No, she was better... safer where she was, cocooned by her inertia... protected by it almost.

Tiredly she lay down on the bed, closing her eyes, her hand resting on the pillow and smoothing the fabric, stroking it as she had once stroked Mitch's skin. Only the pillow felt nothing like Mitch; it was cold, unmoving, unresponsive, inanimate...

Slowly tears started to seep from beneath her closed eyelids.

CHAPTER EIGHT

'No, you are not all right,' Louise expostulated firmly, ignoring Georgia's faint-hearted denials.

They were sitting in Louise's office where Georgia had called to hand in her latest batch of work and collect some more, but after one look at her tense, hunched body and her too pale face Louise had made her sit down in a chair, and had told her that she felt that what Georgia needed was not more work but a good rest.

'But I don't want to rest,' Georgia protested again, adding shakily, 'I can't rest...'

'Then someone will have to make you,' Louise told her, adding in a more gentle voice, 'Georgia, I know how you must be feeling. I remember how I felt when I lost Gran, but making yourself ill won't bring back your aunt. And I know that your getting yourself in this kind of state is the last thing she would want.'

Georgia couldn't speak. She knew that what Louise was saying to her was the truth, and she felt too ashamed to admit to her friend that it wasn't just her aunt's death that was making her feel so depressed, so uncaring of what happened to her. But then how could she tell her friend about that night she had spent with Mitch, about the way she had behaved... the things she had done... said? Even now the memory was enough to make her face start flushing and her body tremble. And the worst thing was that, underneath her shame and guilt, in the night, when her brain was sluggish and unable to control the wanton impulses of her body, she still ached for him . . . still wanted him . . . still cried for him. And even when she did sleep her dreams were vivid and painful, sharp-edged with memories of him, and illogical yearnings for an emotional bonding between them which had never existed.

It had been a fortnight now since her aunt's funeral. Many, many times a day she found herself making a mental note to remember some little incident to relate to her when she visited her at the hospice, only to have to remind herself that there was no point, that her aunt was no longer there to hear her; and yet she often found herself holding imaginary conversations with her, and in some way deriving an odd sort of comfort from doing so, almost a sense of her aunt's presence there actually listening to her . . . soothing her.

Yes, she could think of her aunt, if not with acceptance, then at least with the realisation that her death had been calm and dignified and the way she had wanted it; the loss, the pain, the grief—those were *her* emotions, untainted by any unhappy memories of her aunt's actual death.

But it was when it came to Mitch that her thoughts grew most turbulent and most painful.

When she woke up in the morning she was often actually physically sick with misery and longing.

It was this debilitating sickness that was responsible for her pallor and weight loss, and indirectly for Louise's assertion that she needed to rest and relax and not to work. But she dared not allow herself to stop working. Work was all that stood between her and her almost obsessive need to think about Mitch, to remember how it had felt to touch him ... to be with him ... to love him.

She moved restlessly in her chair, causing Louise to frown.

'Drink your coffee,' Louise suggested, 'and then I'm going to take a couple of hours off and you and I are going to go home and sit in the garden and relax.'

Immediately Georgia started to shake her head, and then stopped. What was the point in trying to argue? Louise plainly meant what she said, and she could no longer claim that she needed to work in order to earn enough money to cover her mortgage payments.

One of her greatest shocks had been the discovery that her aunt had left her quite a considerable sum of money. Money she had carefully saved over the years, by a thousand and one small sacrifices which had never been mentioned, but which, looking back, Georgia could see so plainly and which had brought emotional tears to her eyes when the solicitor had read the will to her.

She had wanted to cry then that there had been no need for her aunt to do without the small luxuries which would have made her life more comfortable in order to leave *her* financially secure. *She* was healthy and young and more than capable of earning her own living. And yet, in the letter she had left her, her aunt had explained that this was something she had wanted to do for her, adding that the bulk of the money had come from the estate of Georgia's own parents, and had been invested and the interest used over the years for such things as school holidays for Georgia, and an allowance when she went to university.

Her aunt's thoughtfulness, her concern, her love, comforting her even when her aunt was no longer there to do so, had caused Georgia to weep fresh tears.

She had already, immediately after Mitch had left, obtained the head office address of his company from Louise and sent him a cheque to cover the rent he had paid her, too proud to want to keep the money he had so carelessly said was not important. Not important to him maybe, but very, very important to her.

'Drink your coffee,' Louise urged.

Obediently Georgia picked up the cup, but the moment the smell of the rich brew reached her nostrils a feeling of such nausea swept over her that she had to put it down, standing up, covering her mouth with her hand, her pallor immediately telling Louise what she was feeling so that the older woman hurried to her side, helping her towards the small cloakroom.

Ten minutes later, when Georgia emerged, she said sympathetically, 'Horrid, isn't it? It must have been the smell of the coffee. I remember when I was pregnant how that affected me...' She broke off as Georgia went even paler, exclaiming, 'Do you still feel sick?'

Georgia shook her head. The nausea was gone. If anything she felt oddly light-headed, almost as though she were floating slightly above the ground, her body empty and hollow. No, it wasn't a renewed bout of nausea which had made her go so pale, but Louise's reference to pregnancy.

'Do you mind if I go straight home?' she said tensely now.

'No, not at all,' Louise assured her. 'But remember what I said. You need to relax and rest...not to work yourself into the ground. Although why I'm saying that to you, when you're just about the best computer programmer we've got on our books, I really don't know...'

Only half listening to her, Georgia picked up her bag, heading for the door.

Her car wasn't parked very far away, but she discovered when she got to it that she was bathed in perspiration, her body trembling inside and out.

Pregnant...she couldn't be, could she? Not after just that one night... Not...

She got into the car and closed her eyes, her thoughts whirling in panic-stricken confusion. Pregnant... How could she be? She wasn't married...wasn't in any kind of committed relationship. The thought of bringing a child into the world, of committing herself to its welfare and upbringing...the very idea of single parenthood was something she had never even contemplated.

A baby...Mitch's baby...

The warm, weakening sensation that spread through her brought emotional tears to her eyes and made her want to laugh and cry at the same time.

Pregnant...she couldn't be. Could she?

*　　*　　*

Several hours later she knew, not only that she *could* be pregnant, but also that she was. She had also known immediately and overpoweringly that, despite all the problems she would encounter, she wanted to have this child . . . Mitch's child.

After all, other women did it. Other women brought up their children single-handedly. All right, so maybe the last thing she had intended when she had so wantonly begged Mitch to make love to her had been to conceive his child. Or had it? Had there, somewhere buried deep in her subconscious, been a desperate need to deny the finality of her aunt's death by creating a new life?

It was perhaps a fanciful, even stupid thought . . . the kind of thought a pregnant woman might be expected to have, but a thought nevertheless that she could not deny. After all, she wasn't a naïve girl; she had known the consequences of what she was doing. Mitch himself had warned her, and she had ignored that warning . . . and not just ignored it, but deliberately allowed him to think . . . Her body tightened suddenly.

The baby . . . his baby, would be entirely hers. Mitch himself could never know about it, would not want to know. After all, when they made love he had merely been responding to her sexually with no thought in his mind of creating a new life.

But a new life *had* been created. A life for her to nurture and cherish . . . a child . . . his child. The aching, quickening, softening sensation within that that knowledge brought made her tremble anew.

At the place where she had gone to have her own test confirmed, they had advised her impartially. Should she wish to have a termination...

She had known then that, no matter how illogical, how emotional, how un-thought-out her immediate response to that suggestion had been, her decision had been made. Even though up until now the thought of a child, especially a child who would be her sole responsibility, had been something she had never even contemplated, now that she was pregnant her strongest, most powerful urge had been a need to protect that new life she was carrying. Not because of her aunt, not even because the child was Mitch's, but because it was there... because it demanded her protection, her nurture, her love, for its own sake.

Pregnant... She was, she realised as she heard the impatient hooting of a car horn behind her, blocking the other traffic, lost in the bemusement of her own thoughts.

It was early evening before she was rational enough to dwell on all the practical aspects of her pregnancy. It could not be kept a secret, of course, nor did she want it to be... but Mitch's role as her child's father... that must be... She might have the right to bear her child, to love it and want it, but she did not have the right to inflict an unwanted child on its father, even had she wanted to do so, which she did not. But people were bound to be curious...Louise especially. Her friend would quite naturally want to know.

But not yet... not now. For now she hoped that her friend would simply accept that the father of her child was someone she did not want to discuss.

As she sat by the kitchen table, nursing the mug of herbal tea she had made for herself in place of her normal coffee, she found herself wishing that her aunt were alive to share this moment with her, knowing that the older woman would not have sat in judgement or condemned her. Knowing how much she would have loved the baby.

That night she dreamed of Mitch again. In her dream he had found out about the baby and he was angry with her, telling her that it was all her fault... that she should never have allowed herself to conceive, that, had the decision been his, he would never have agreed to her having his child.

When she woke up, her heart was pounding and she was cold; there were tears on her face, and panic and pain in her heart. No, Mitch must never find out about the baby, she told herself as she sat up in bed, shivering, hugging her arms protectively around her knees.

It was just as well he had gone back to London. She hoped he stayed there. For the sake of her child she *wanted* him to stay there. For the sake of her child she never wanted to see him again, never wanted him to see... to realise...

She bit back a half-hysterical laugh. If by some mischance he did return... if he did decide to transfer his head office to the town... if they should meet and he should realise that she was pregnant... if he should question the paternity of her child, she would just have to pretend her baby's father was the non-existent married lover with whom he had believed her to be having an affair.

Outside it had started to rain, but the sound comforted her, reminding her of the roses she had ordered as she had promised her aunt.

One day, when he or she was old enough to understand, she would tell her child about the roses and about her aunt.

And would she tell him or her about Mitch? Unwilling to answer such a question, she settled back beneath the bedclothes and closed her eyes.

Where before she had been careless of her health, uncaring of whether or not she ate or slept properly, now for the baby's sake she forced herself to eat the breakfast she would normally have forgone, reminding herself that her baby needed the nutrition even if she felt more nauseous than appreciative of her bowl of cereal and milk.

It amazed her how calm she felt, how full of purpose and determination; how charged with a new energy for life, a new purposefulness.

When she arrived at Louise's office a little later in the day and announced that she wanted to get back to work, Louise immediately started to remonstrate with her.

'I need the work, and the money,' Georgia told her, adding quietly, 'I'm pregnant, Louise.'

As she had expected, her friend was stunned at first, but not in the least disapproving or critical, asking only, 'I won't ask if you're sure this is what you want. I can see that it is, although I must admit I didn't realise...'

'It wasn't planned,' Georgia interrupted her quickly. 'An... an accident, in fact. To be honest, until you mentioned pregnancy the other morning, it hadn't even occurred to me that I could be pregnant.'

'And the father,' Louise questioned her, 'is he... will he...?'

'He doesn't know, nor do I want him to know,' Georgia told her. She saw her friend's expression and added shakily, 'He wouldn't want to know, Louise. I can't go into all the circumstances. The fact that I am pregnant is my responsibility, my fault if you like... something that happened in... in a moment of madness almost. Something I hadn't planned on or ever imagined could happen to me; but now that it has... I want this baby,' she told her fiercely. 'I just wish Aunt May were still alive.'

'Well, I can't pretend that you haven't surprised me,' Louise admitted, 'but these days for a woman to bring up a child on her own is nothing out of the ordinary.'

It was over an hour before Georgia left Louise's office armed with enough work to keep her going for the rest of the week. Just as she was leaving, Louise told her, 'I know it's rather selfish of me, but I'm rather relieved that you came in. Mitch Fletcher's PA was on the phone this morning asking me if we could find them some more temps, and without you taking this stuff off my hands I'd have been hard put to it to supply them with people of the right calibre. I was dying to ask her if it's known yet whether or not Mitch intends to transfer his main operation down here, but of course it's the kind of thing you just can't ask, and, even if I had, I doubt if she would have told me anything. She's one of the old school, late fifties, widowed, I believe, and intensely loyal to her boss.'

Fortunately Georgia had her back to Louise. Even so, she was terrified that the tension in her body might inadvertently betray her. Certainly she knew that it was impossible for her to even utter Mitch's name without her voice starting to tremble, and so she ignored her friend's comment, instead opening the door and saying huskily, 'I'll let you have this lot back just as soon as I can.'

Her next port of call was the building society, where she wrote the cheque that would clear her mortgage with an immense sense of relief.

Yet another reason for her to be grateful to Aunt May, she reflected a little weepily once she had left. It was true that she could probably have managed, had she sold the cottage and bought something smaller, somewhere closer to town without a garden . . . somewhere where her child would be denied the healthy surroundings of the cottage. But she herself would certainly have been under a good deal more stress and anxiety without her aunt's unexpected legacy. As it was, she knew now that if for any reason she felt unable to work during her pregnancy, or perhaps it took her longer to get back to work than she hoped after the baby's arrival, then she would not have to panic about how she was going to live in the meantime.

She went to the supermarket, shopping carefully, mindful now of the importance of eating well and healthily.

In the morning she had an appointment with her doctor. He was their local GP and had attended her aunt before the latter had opted to go into the hospice. Georgia wasn't quite sure how he was going to react to her pregnancy, or how many questions he would ask her about her baby's father. Whatever he did ask her, she was determined to keep Mitch's identity a secret. She owed him that much at least. After all, he had not asked to be the father of her child, and she was quite certain it was not what he would have wanted—quite, quite certain.

She need not have worried: although she stumbled a little over her words when she explained to her doctor the reasons for her desire to keep her baby's father's identity a secret, he made no attempt to push her into changing her mind, concentrating instead on discussing with her her own state of health, warning her that she was underweight, reminding her that she had been under a considerable amount of stress, and that the early weeks of a pregnancy could be very, very vulnerable ones for the newly forming foetus.

'Are you saying that I could lose my baby?' Georgia asked him anxiously.

'Not necessarily. I'm simply pointing out to you that because of the stress you've been under, and the fact that your own mental and physical reserves have been depleted by your aunt's illness, you must be prepared to be extra-specially vigilant and make sure you don't overtire yourself.' He frowned a little. 'You're rather remote where you live. I hope I don't need to warn you against the dangers of climbing stepladders, and dashing up and down stairs without looking where you're going. I don't normally advocate women doing anything other than leading a normal life during pregnancy, but in your case...' He shook his head slightly. 'You wouldn't believe the number of my pregnant patients who seem overwhelmed by a compulsion to start decorating. If you get that kind of urge—don't!'

Georgia looked uncertainly at him. Was he trying to tell her that her baby was at risk in some way, or was he simply trying to caution her against overdoing things?

As though he had read her mind he said gently, 'Nothing's wrong, Georgia. Both you and your baby will be fine, just as long as you remember to take proper care of yourself. You obviously want this baby.'

'Very much,' Georgia assured him fervently.

'Good.' He smiled at her. 'We have a regular clinic for our mothers-to-be, and there are all manner of other activities as well. Natural childbirth classes, swimming classes... Heather, our receptionist, will give you all the details.'

When she got home, Georgia started on the work Louise had given her. When she realised that it was work for Mitch's company, her heart started to beat too fast, and her hands trembled unsteadily.

Mitch... Where was he now? What was he doing? Who was he with? Did he ever think about her at all...?

Stop that right now, she warned herself shakily. It was pointless letting her thoughts travel down paths which ought to remain closed to them.

She had expected, hoped that with the baby to distract her she would cease having such vivid dreams about Mitch; that she would cease aching for him, wondering about him, loving him... but instead it was almost as though having conceived his child had strengthened her unwanted emotional bonding with him.

It was ridiculous for a woman of her age to have fallen in love with a man on the strength of such a short period of knowing him, especially when he had done nothing to encourage her to do so. If she hadn't begged him so wantonly to make love to her that night, would she ever have realised how she felt about him? Or would she simply have gone on believing that all the emotion he generated inside her was caused by resentment and dislike? It was too late to ask herself that question now. She did love him, and even if she could she would not have wished that night with him away. Her hand touched her stomach, a tender smile curling her mouth as she thought of her child. Mitch's child...

She was six months pregnant, and the baby was just beginning to show in a small but unmistakable bulge beneath her clothes, when she heard the devastating news that Mitch was after all moving his headquarters from London to their town.

It was, of course, Louise who gave her the news. For a while Georgia had wondered if Louise had guessed that Mitch was the father of her child, but then she had told herself that she was being over-sensitive and that Louise simply mentioned him so often because she was thinking of the difference it would make to her business if he did move his main operation to the town.

'It's official, too. Apparently he's been in nego-tiation with the local council and the planning people about the feasibility of extending the factory and building a new office block, and now it's all got the go-ahead.

'Saul was saying that he'd heard on the grapevine that Mitch is looking for a house in the area. Apparently he's moving back into the hotel in the meantime.'

Georgia dared not look at her in case she gave herself away. She was conscious of a strong need to be on her own to come to terms with what she had just learned. Mitch, moving permanently into the area. How was she going to feel? How was she going to react if she should happen to bump into him accidentally in the town? How was she going to be able to cover up her feelings . . . her love . . . ?

She took her leave of Louise as quickly as she could, needing to be on her own to come to terms with what she had learned.

Mitch as someone living far away in London, where she did not have to see him, where it was only in her dreams, her wayward thoughts, her heart that she had to cope with the pain of loving him, was one thing; Mitch in person, here in her own environment, here in the town where their child would be born and would grow up, was quite another.

So far she had been lucky. All the few people who knew about the baby had respected her desire to keep its father a secret.

To Louise she had confided that the baby's conception had been an accident; that its father did not love her.

'Although you love him,' Louise had shrewdly guessed, and Georgia had not been able to deny it, even though caution urged her that she should.

Now she would have to be doubly careful to make sure that no one came anywhere near guessing that Mitch was the father of her child. A tiny tremor ran through her. But what if Mitch himself should guess...should ask...? Would she be strong enough to lie to him, to deny that the child was his?

That evening, for the first time since she had found out about her pregnancy, she felt unable to eat her evening meal.

She was, so her doctor had repeatedly warned her, still a little underweight, the months of her aunt's illness having taken a toll on her which still left its mark.

Her grief for her aunt had softened a little now, although with Christmas so short a time away she couldn't help thinking of her childhood Christmases which her aunt had made so very special for her. Her aunt might no longer be there to share the season with her, but the traditions she had enjoyed so much could be carried on by her, Georgia, for her own child, and that way Aunt May could live in her child's imagination as well as in her own mind.

She would, just as Aunt May had always done, have a real tree...not a small apology of a tree, either, but a lovely large bushy one which she would decorate with all the traditional things her aunt had always used.

Busily she planned, knowing by now that when she felt like this, when she ached with loneliness and longed for her aunt to be there with her, the best way of coping with that feeling was to keep her mind and her body active.

She only wished she could get over loving Mitch in the same way, but she had years of shared memories of love and caring of her aunt to sustain her through her loss of her, while she had virtually nothing of Mitch, only a few whispered words, a night full of caresses...and the heartache of knowing that she loved him while to him she meant nothing at all.

Every time she remembered the speed with which he had left her even before she was awake, she felt sick inside with misery and self-disgust, and yet she knew that, given the time over again, she would not change anything.

Her hand touched the firm swell of her belly with tender love.

And most especially she would not change this...that she had conceived Mitch's child.

CHAPTER NINE

'WHAT is it? What's wrong?' Georgia demanded anxiously as she looked from the nurse's frowning face to the midwife's. Normally she enjoyed her antenatal visits, but today for some reason she had been gently ushered away from the other mothers without any explanation being given.

Now she felt her heart start to race as fear for her child filled her.

'Nothing's wrong,' the young midwife firmly soothed her. 'It's just that your baby doesn't seem to be growing quite as fast as he or she should. It does happen sometimes that for one reason or another a baby does stop growing. Normally it's just a temporary thing, but... well, we do like to keep a special check when it does happen, and you are still a little underweight...'

Guilt filled Georgia. If anything happened to her baby through her neglect...

'What will I have to do... what will happen?' she demanded anxiously.

'Nothing at this stage,' the midwife soothed her, 'but what I would like you to do is to come back in a week's time. If your baby still isn't showing any signs of growing then...' Her frown deepened, causing Georgia to feel as though her heart were actually turning over inside her.

'What can I do?' she begged.

'Rest and eat properly,' the midwife told her promptly.

'And if my baby hasn't started to grow again when I come in next week...'

The midwife paused and then said quietly, 'We'll have to see. It may mean admitting you here to the hospital where we can keep an eye on both of you... but let's not get too alarmed too soon. As I said, this kind of thing does happen. A temporary rest on the part of the baby... At this stage there's no need for you to panic. In fact it's the last thing you should do,' she stressed firmly.

When Georgia left the hospital half an hour later, she was still in a state of shock. She walked blindly along the pavement, oblivious to the presence of the man watching her from the other side of the road. Her baby was at risk, and it was her fault. It had to be. If anything... Panic and guilt started to fill her. She had never felt more alone or more afraid in her life.

She thought of going to see Louise to pour out her worry to her friend, but then she remembered that Louise was preparing for the arrival of both her own and Saul's parents who were spending Christmas with them, and she felt she could not inflict herself on her friend at such a busy time.

As she drove home she was miserably aware of a great searing fear, a loneliness... Tears started to fill her eyes, but she blinked them away. Self-pity wasn't what she needed right now. Self-pity would get her nowhere and would do nothing to help her baby. She had known, when she'd made the decision to have her baby, that the two of them would be alone both during her pregnancy and afterwards; that there would be no one for her to share the experience with, no husband...no lover...no close family even. She had known that and had felt that she would be strong enough to cope. Was she now saying that she wasn't?

Immediately her body tensed as she rejected such a thought. It was just the shock, the unexpectedness of what she had been told...the feeling of fear and guilt that she herself was somehow responsible for what was happening to her baby...that it was suffering because of her.

When she got home she parked her car and walked tiredly into the kitchen. She knew she ought to eat, but the thought of having to prepare a meal, a meal she would then sit down to and eat completely alone, made her feel more tired and depressed than ever. The heating was on and yet she still felt cold. Coming home through the town she had seen into homes where Christmas trees were already decorated and lit up; had envisaged the happy and excited family scenes going on in those homes and had contrasted them with her own aloneness.

Now, at a time when she was least able to cope with it, she was conscious of a great welling need for Mitch...a terrible feeling of despair and misery...a huge yawning emptiness in her life that only he could fill.

When she heard the doorbell ring, the sound was so unexpected that it was several seconds before she bothered to move.

Who on earth would be visiting her at this time in the evening? Probably someone wanting to sell something, she told herself wearily as she walked into the hall and switched on the light.

She opened the door cautiously, and then froze, exclaiming disbelievingly, 'M-Mitch!'

'Are you on your own?'

She stared at him in confusion, the shock of seeing him so unexpectedly robbing her of any ability to think logically.

'Yes... Yes, I'm on my own,' she confirmed as he came in.

'So he hasn't moved in with you then, despite this?' he demanded tersely, his glance falling to the unmistakable swell of her belly. 'Did you do it deliberately, Georgia? Did you conceive this child in the hope that it would make him leave his wife for you?' he asked her roughly.

Her mouth had gone dry, her throat muscles paralysed by the shock of what he was saying to her.

'I saw you in town this afternoon,' she heard him saying to her. 'I couldn't believe it at first. Couldn't believe that you would ever be so... so...'

'So careless,' Georgia supplied for him, as her shock started to recede and a volatile mixture of anguish, pain and anger took its place. Had she really thought for one emotional moment when she'd opened the door to him that somehow he had guessed the truth and, having guessed it, had come here to claim both her and his child... to tell her that he loved her, that he loved *them*... that he wanted them? Because if so... if she had actually been that foolish, it was being brought home to her now just how criminally stupid she had been.

His mouth she saw now had folded in a grimly uncompromising line.

'Were you merely careless, Georgia?'

His words were like the cruellest of blows raining down on her unprotected heart, each one more devastatingly painful than the last. Was that what he really thought: that she had deliberately chosen to become pregnant by her married lover, in the hope that by doing so she would force him to leave his wife and family?

There was a sour taste in her mouth, a dark bitterness around her heart. Did he really have so low an opinion of her?

When she didn't answer him he pressed her relentlessly, 'But he isn't here with you, is he? He's betrayed you, just as he betrayed his wife. Did you really think...?' He stopped and then demanded curtly, 'And now you're pregnant and the father of your child has deserted you... has deserted both of you, hasn't he?'

Georgia raised her head and forced herself to look at him.

'Yes, I suppose in a manner of speaking he has,' she agreed quietly, still in shock, unable to either deny what he was saying or tell him the truth.

An odd expression crossed his face; anger was there, irritation and bewilderment too, and there was also something else... something almost approaching pain, although why her words should cause *him* pain she had no idea, unless it was because they reminded him of something from his own childhood, his own father's cruel treatment both of him and his mother.

'And yet still you don't blame him, do you?' He said it almost accusingly, watching her.

Slowly Georgia shook her head. 'For what?' she demanded huskily. 'For the fact that I have conceived his child?' Her head lifted proudly. 'The option to go ahead with the pregnancy, the decision to go ahead with it was mine. It was my choice; my wish. I want this child.'

'Even though both you and it have been deserted by its father?' he asked her grimly.

'There are worse things in life for a child to endure than not having a father,' Georgia pointed out gently to him. She saw from the expression in his eyes that he knew exactly what she meant. 'This child... my child will never doubt that I love it.'

She turned on her heel as she spoke, intending to make it plain to him that she wanted him to leave, afraid that if he stayed much longer, forcing her to discuss such an emotive subject, she was bound to give herself away. He already despised her, and she could imagine how he would feel if he knew that he was the father of her child... how he would deny her, deny them both.

As her emotions rose up inside her, panicking her, she moved clumsily, catching her heel in the fringe of a rug on the kitchen floor. It was something she had done a dozen or more times before, each time swearing that she would move the rug or get rid of it altogether and then forgetting until the next time, but this time the combined shock of Mitch's arrival, plus her natural fear for her baby, made her tense as she felt herself falling forward, and cry out in sharp panic as she realised what was happening.

Mitch moved quickly, but not quickly enough to save her, and as he knelt over her prone body, asking her if she was all right, the only thing she could think of was her baby, tears filling her eyes.

'Don't worry, you're going to be fine,' she heard Mitch assuring her, and then before she could stop him he was gently helping her to her feet, supporting her weight against him, guiding her gently to a chair once he was sure she felt strong enough to move. 'Stay there,' he told her grimly. 'I'm going to ring for a doctor.'

Georgia wanted to protest that she didn't need his help, but she was too afraid for her baby to do or say anything, numbly telling him where he would find her doctor's number while she sat trembling in the chair, willing her tense muscles to relax, her mind begging over and over again for there to be no ill effects from her fall.

She felt sick and light-headed, her stomach churning nauseously.

It was just shock, she told herself—just shock, that was all—but all the time she was desperately conscious of the warning they had given her at the hospital and of how fragile and precious the new life inside her was.

During the half-hour it took for the doctor to arrive, Mitch paced up and down the kitchen, watching her with eyes that warned her not to even attempt to move.

Oddly enough his tension helped to ease a little of her own fear. What a difference it made having someone with her sharing the waiting, sharing her anxiety... Would he be equally anxious if he knew that it was his child she was carrying? She gave a small shudder which he saw, instantly coming to her side and demanding tersely, 'What is it? What's wrong?'

'Nothing,' she lied. 'I just felt a bit cold, that's all.'

She thought from the way he frowned at her that he must have guessed she had lied, but the next minute he was opening the kitchen door and walking into the hall. She heard him going upstairs and when he came down again he was carrying the quilt from her bed, which he then proceeded to tuck round her.

When his fingers accidently brushed against the hard mound of her belly she flinched and then trembled. Tears were pricking dangerously at the back of her eyes. If only things were different, if only he loved her... if only he wanted their child as much as she did.

He was watching her, she realised, his eyes hard and grim, but before he could say anything they both heard the sound of the car drawing up outside.

'That will be the doctor,' she said unnecessarily.

'You stay there. I'll go and let him in,' Mitch told her.

'Well, now, what have you been doing to yourself?' her doctor asked her cheerfully when he came into the kitchen.

Quickly she explained what had happened, watching his smile turn to a frown as he turned to Mitch and said quietly, 'I think it would be better if she was upstairs in bed. If you could...'

Although she wanted to protest that she was perfectly capable of walking upstairs unaided, it seemed easier to give in and let Mitch support the weight of her body, one arm wrapped firmly round her, his other hand holding on to her as he guided her upstairs.

Pregnancy had heightened some of her senses, especially that of smell, and the scent of him when she was so close to him overwhelmed her with an agonising mixture of pain and joy. She wanted to close her eyes and lean against him for ever, to simply melt into him and be a part of him... to be absorbed so fully and completely by him that she could never again be separate from him. She could feel weak tears of emotion burning behind her closed eyelids and faltered in mid-step as she tried to control her emotional weakness.

Instantly Mitch stopped moving, exclaiming tautly.

'Georgia... what is it? What's wrong?'

She shook her head, unable to speak, knowing that if she didn't put some distance between them soon she was likely to break down completely.

Her hand touched her stomach as she felt the baby move inside her as though it too wanted to be closer to him. In her heart she whispered a plea to it that it would understand and forgive her for denying it its right to know and love its father, telling it that it was for its sake that she did so, so that it would not suffer Mitch's rejection.

Thankfully they were upstairs now and it wasn't far to her room.

'I'm going to get the midwife to come out and take a look at you,' the doctor was saying as Mitch went downstairs for her quilt. 'I suspect she'll agree with me that you're going to need a couple of weeks' bed-rest.'

Mitch came back into the bedroom just in time to catch what the doctor was saying to her. At first, Georgia didn't see him, panic flooding through her as she heard what her doctor said.

'A couple of weeks... but I can't...'

'I'm afraid you're going to have to,' her doctor told her firmly. 'In fact what I'd like to do is to take you into hospital where we can keep a proper eye on you, but we just don't have the spare beds, although...' He paused, frowning a little, and Georgia's body started to shake.

Was he trying to say that her baby was at risk? She started to ask him, her panic showing in her voice.

'After that kind of fall, there's always some element of risk,' he told her quietly. 'And in your case we have the added problem of the baby ceasing to grow.'

Georgia wished that Mitch would go away. She was acutely conscious of him standing beside the bed, listening to every word the doctor was saying, the frown on his forehead deepening, the look in his eyes as he turned to study her making her feel as though he felt that she was deliberately and wantonly risking her baby's health.

Why was he doing it? Why was he staying? After all, none of this had anything to do with him; at least not so far as he was aware, and yet he still refused to go, even when the midwife finally arrived. And even though she was desperately afraid of him staying because having him there made her feel so emotionally vulnerable, at the same time there was a sharply painful joy in him being there, in feeling that she was no longer alone. She shivered, telling herself that it was dangerous for her to allow herself to feel like that...that, whatever feelings of concern and human kindness were inclining him to stay, he would soon be gone.

When the midwife arrived, she repeated what the doctor had already said: that Georgia must have at least one and preferably two weeks of bed-rest. Georgia tried to protest that that was impossible, but the midwife frowned at her and told her almost tersely, 'I'm afraid for your baby's sake that you're going to have to make it possible.'

And then she was getting up, telling Georgia that she would be back to see her in the morning and that in the meantime she was not to worry but to get as much rest as she could.

Mitch had gone downstairs while the midwife was examining her, but once she and the doctor had gone he came back up to her room.

She was undressed and in bed now and it made her feel acutely vulnerable to have him standing beside her bed, looking at her with that grave look on his face.

'I'm going into town now to collect my stuff from the hotel. I shan't be long—an hour...will you be all right?'

What did he mean...what was he talking about? Georgia stared at him in confusion.

'There's no need for you to come back,' she told him shakily. 'I'm grateful to you for what you've done, but...'

'But if it hadn't been for me, it would never have happened,' he finished for her.

For a moment she was too shocked to speak. So he did know after all...had somehow guessed.

'If it hadn't been for me, you would never have tripped on that damn rug,' she heard him saying grimly, and she realised that he was not blaming himself for her pregnancy at all, simply for her fall.

'It wasn't your fault,' she told him dully. 'I should have thrown that rug out. It was kind of you to stay while...while the doctor was here...but there's really no need for you to come back.'

'On the contrary, there's every need,' he corrected her grimly. 'The doctor told me that you were not to be left alone. Complete bed-rest is what you need...and that means you have to stay in bed. And for that you need someone here with you.'

Georgia sat up in bed and stared at him. 'But you can't do that!'

'Meaning you'd rather go into hospital, providing of course that they can find you a bed... Unless of course your lover is going to change his mind and move in here with you; but to do that he would have to desert his existing family, wouldn't he?'

Georgia raised her hands to her ears. 'Stop it . . . stop it!' she told him shakily. She just wasn't equipped to deal with this, especially not now. Her body ached all over, she felt emotionally and physically exhausted, and added to her own physical discomfort was her fear for her baby. The last thing she felt capable of doing right now was arguing with anyone, much less Mitch.

Instantly he was at her side, sitting on the edge of the bed, catching hold of her hands, his touch so tender, so warm and gentle that it made her start to tremble with aching longing.

'I'm sorry, I didn't mean to upset you, but the doctor and the midwife both stressed to me how important it is that you rest.'

'They stressed to you . . .' Georgia said painfully. 'But why . . . ?'

She could see the tension in his face as he dropped his hands from hers and stood up.

'They seemed to assume that the baby was mine,' he told her curtly.

Georgia felt faint and sick; a huge wave of weakness seemed to roll right over her. Had they guessed, then? Had she said or done something while Mitch was there which had betrayed the truth to them?

'You should have told them it isn't,' she said quickly. 'You . . .'

'Perhaps I should, but I was more concerned for your health and the baby's than putting right what was after all a perfectly understandable mistake.'

His lack of concern totally astounded her. She would have expected him to object strenuously to any implication that he was the father of her child, and yet here he was treating it as though it didn't bother him in the least.

'I'm going now,' he told her. 'But I shan't be long.'

'There's no need for you to come back,' Georgia started to protest again, but he was already halfway through the door and heading for the stairs.

When she heard the front door close behind him and then his car engine start, she told herself that when he came back she would have to find a way of convincing him that there was no need for him to stay. Frustratedly she wished there were someone . . . a friend . . . anyone she could call on to come and stay with her instead, but there was no one apart from Louise, and she could hardly impose on her like that so close to Christmas.

Tears started to fill her eyes. It was bad enough that Mitch thought so badly of her; that she was now going to be forced to have him living with her again, daily, hourly tormented by his proximity while at the same time knowing that he didn't want her . . . didn't love her . . .

She moved uncomfortably in her bed. Perhaps if she could prove to him that she didn't need him; that she could cope on her own . . .

She pushed back the bedclothes and swung her feet to the ground; the dizziness that filled her made her steady herself nervously on the edge of the bed as she struggled to stand upright.

She felt so weak, so shaky . . . terrified almost to take a step in case she fell and hurt her baby.

As she stood there trembling, willing herself to take first one step and then another, she acknowledged how frightened she was.

She made it as far as the bathroom, but once she got there she felt so weak that she had to sit down for several minutes before she was able to make her way back to her bedroom.

It was only when she was safely back in her bed, her body trembling with tension and weakness, that she acknowledged how impossible it actually was for her to cope on her own.

Her fall had thoroughly unnerved her, and, coming on top of the midwife's warning that the baby seemed to have stopped growing, it had the effect of making her feel so nervous and afraid that she knew that really the last thing she wanted was to be in the house on her own.

Had she had close neighbours it wouldn't have been so bad, and she knew that if Louise knew what was happening her friend would immediately insist on her moving into her home. But how could she do that? She knew also that Louise had her hands full with both sets of visiting parents.

What would she have done if Mitch hadn't been there to step into the breach? She suspected that, had that been the case, the midwife would have insisted on admitting her to hospital.

She wasn't sure which was the more potentially unwanted alternative: having Mitch living in the house with her, or spending the next week or so in hospital. On balance, she reflected that she would almost have preferred to be in hospital, but then she remembered how short they were of beds and how her admission would take up a bed that might be needed by a far more urgent emergency case. How would she feel if someone was prevented from getting the care they needed because of her selfishness in being too afraid of revealing her feelings to Mitch to accept his offer of help?

What she still could not understand was *why* he had offered to stay with her. After all, why should he care what happened to her? He had seemed to intimate earlier that he believed he was responsible for her fall. Certainly it was his presence in the cottage, and the argument she had been having with him, that had led to her clumsiness... but as to her fall being his fault...

She stiffened as she heard the sound of a car returning. Surely he wasn't back already? She felt panic begin to churn inside her. How was she going to cope with hiding her feelings... her love? Would her pride be strong enough to prevent her from revealing how she felt about him? It would have to be, she told herself desperately as she heard him coming upstairs.

She looked at her alarm clock. He had been just over an hour.

When he walked into the bedroom, he stopped and looked at her, almost as though he had been half expecting not to find her in her bed, she recognised, as she saw the way his muscles relaxed a little.

'I've brought you some fruit,' he told her. 'I wasn't sure if you had any particular preference...'

The basket he was carrying was not an ornate shop-filled one, but one in which a veritable cornucopia of exotic and expensive fruits had been piled so high that he needed both hands to balance it.

Foolish emotional tears started to cloud her eyes as she stared at it. How long was it since anyone had done something like this for her? It wasn't the expense of the fruit, although one look at what he had brought told her that it had been expensive, that the fruits were out of season, and what was more that they had the kind of firm ripeness which meant he could only have bought them from the town's most exclusive supermarket. No, it was the fact that he had thought about buying them for her and then had so obviously chosen them for her himself. When her aunt was alive they would often indulge one another with small treats of favourite foods, and fresh flowers, but this was the first time that a man . . . She swallowed hard. Not just a man, but the man . . . the man she loved and wanted . . . the man who . . . Her hand touched her stomach and immediately, as though something in her gesture held some special significance for him, Mitch's eyes darkened, his gaze fixed on her body.

'I'm just going downstairs to make us both some supper,' he announced harshly. 'The doctor told me that you're underweight and need to eat more.'

'Please, there's no need for you to do all this for me,' Georgia protested huskily.

'It's no trouble. After all, if I'm going to cook for myself, cooking for two instead of one isn't any problem.'

'But why . . . why are you doing this?' Georgia asked him dazedly, unable to hold back the question which had been puzzling her ever since he announced that he intended to move back into the cottage.

'Someone has to,' he told her curtly. 'And I don't see your lover leaving his wife and moving in here, do you? Or is that still what you're hoping for, just as you...?'

'Just as I what?' Georgia demanded, and started to tremble as she remembered the argument they had been having in the kitchen earlier. 'Just as I deliberately allowed myself to get pregnant? It wasn't like that!'

She could hear the emotion in her own voice, the tears that weren't so very far away, even though she warned herself that getting so worked up wasn't good either for herself or far more importantly for the baby either...

Mitch obviously must have been thinking along the same lines because he backtracked quickly...too quickly for his words to be genuine, Georgia felt as he told her,

'No, of course...I should never have implied... I'm sorry if I upset you. It was just the shock of seeing you and realising... I'll go down and make our supper...'

He had gone before she could say anything to him. When he came back, she would try to speak to him again, to tell him that she didn't need him here with her, she assured herself valiantly, even while a part of her acknowledged that she was deliberately deceiving herself; that there was nothing she wanted more than to have him here in the cottage with her, no matter how dangerous or disturbing his presence might be.

But if he stayed she would be in danger of allowing herself to become enmeshed in impossible daydreams, daydreams in which he wasn't simply staying with her out of some misplaced sense of responsibility and humanity but because he *wanted* to be with her... because he loved her... because he wanted both her and their child to be a part of his life.

She moved restlessly beneath the bedclothes, angry with herself for allowing her thoughts to stray down such forbidden paths.

She could hear him moving about downstairs. Food was the last thing she wanted, she told herself tetchily, unwilling to acknowledge that her irritation came not so much because she didn't want to eat, but because she would have preferred him to stay with her, talking to her...

Talking to her? Insulting her, didn't she mean, with his assumptions about her... assumptions which were completely unfounded and incorrect... assumptions which...? She tensed as she heard him coming back upstairs.

When he opened the bedroom door and she caught the richly fragrant smell of the spaghetti bolognese he had made for her, she was suddenly so hungry that she was sitting up in bed and reaching for the tray he was holding out to her before she realised what she was doing.

'No coffee,' he told her reprovingly, handing her a cup of herbal tea instead. 'It's bad for the baby— too much caffeine.'

Georgia was too interested in the spaghetti to argue with him. Heavens, it smelled good... so good that she couldn't wait to tuck into it. She realised that he was watching her and asked him, 'Where's yours?'

There was a small pause. He was, she realised, looking at her in an oddly assessing fashion, as though he was trying to work out something that did not quite add up.

'Downstairs,' he answered her question. 'I thought you'd prefer to eat on your own.'

Immediately her face flushed. What a stupid thing for her to have said. Of course he wouldn't be eating up here with her. Why on earth had she been so stupid, so...so unguarded...?

'Yes...yes, I do,' she lied.

He was opening her bedroom door and she had to bite hard on her bottom lip to stop herself from pleading with him to stay.

When he had gone downstairs she asked herself shakily how, if she was like this already after so short a space of time, she was going to cope with having him here for a whole fortnight.

The best thing she could do was to get herself back to full health just as soon as she could. After all, the less time he was here, the less she would be at risk of betraying to him how she felt.

And yet, even as the thought formed, she was filled with panic at the thought of him leaving...of being without him.

CHAPTER TEN

'GOODNESS me, Mitch is spoiling you, isn't he?' Louise commented, surveying the fruit and glossy magazines piled up on the bedside table.

Georgia had been forced to ring her to explain what had happened and why she was not able to take on any fresh work, and of course Louise had immediately announced that she was coming round to see her.

'Well, at least the baby's started to grow again,' Georgia told her, ignoring her comment about Mitch and hoping that Louise hadn't noticed the way her skin had flushed at the mention of his name.

'Yes, that is good news, but Mitch was saying that both the doctor and the midwife think your weight is still too low and they're insisting that you've still got to rest. It was lucky Mitch was here when you fell.' She started to frown. 'If you'd been here on your own...'

'Well, I wasn't,' Georgia told her quickly. Even now, a week after the event, she still hated thinking about what could have happened if she had fallen while she was on her own. She knew from comments that Mitch had made to her that he blamed himself for the accident, even though she had pointed out to him that the rug's presence on the kitchen floor was her responsibility and not his. She wondered sometimes if it was guilt that had made him insist on staying with her, and suspected that it must have been.

To her astonishment he had even announced that he intended to work from the cottage, so that he was virtually there with her twenty-four hours a day.

Louise had been with her for less than an hour when he came upstairs, firmly reminding them both that she was supposed to be resting.

Louise got up immediately, ignoring Georgia's protests that there was nothing wrong with her now and no reason why she should still be languishing in bed.

'The doctor says you're to stay there at least until the end of the week,' Mitch reminded her grimly. 'And that's exactly what you are going to do.'

When they had both gone downstairs she told herself she was staying in bed not because Mitch had insisted on it, but because she knew it was what was best for her baby, even if sometimes she did get impatient and want to be up and about and doing things.

Christmas was getting so close. Mitch would be gone before then, of course. She gave a tiny shiver, unwilling to admit how much she was dreading him leaving.

From downstairs she could hear the rise and fall of Mitch's and Louise's voices, and she wondered a little jealously just what it was they were finding to talk about before pushing her feeling aside, telling herself that she was being ridiculous. As she should be the first to admit, Mitch was one of those rare men who actually seemed to enjoy talking to women, treating them as intellectual equals. In the evenings now when he came to collect her empty tray, he spent longer and longer in her room, chatting with her. The range of subjects they had covered amazed her and she knew that, even if she hadn't loved him, she would miss him when he left as a companion and someone who, given different circumstances, could have become a good and true friend.

Aunt May would have liked him. She felt tears start to prick her eyes. Her aunt was never far away from her thoughts. She had already ordered the roses she intended to plant; the roses her aunt had particularly wanted.

It was a long time before she heard Louise drive away. Despite the fact that she kept on insisting to both Mitch and the midwife that she was perfectly well enough to get up now, she knew she was still not back to her full strength. The midwife had allowed her to get up and go downstairs for a few hours every afternoon from the beginning of the week, but she seemed to tire so easily. Because her growing baby was making so many demands on her body, the midwife had told her, reminding her that she was still underweight.

She heard Mitch coming upstairs and frowned as she glanced at her watch. It was too early for lunch yet, and Mitch normally spent the mornings working. Today Louise's visit had interrupted that routine, but Georgia still had no idea what had brought him upstairs.

When he opened her bedroom door, he looked grim-faced, shocked almost. He came into the room and closed the door behind him, and, as he approached the bed, for some reason a faint *frisson* of alarm shivered down Georgia's spine.

She had never seen him looking like this before...so...so close-faced and withdrawn. Was he going to tell her that he had changed his mind and that he had decided to leave? Had he guessed after all...? He and Louise had been talking for a long time... Had her friend said something to him that...?

'Louise has just been telling me about your aunt,' he announced flatly.

Georgia's heart pounded heavily with shock and then started racing frantically as he continued, 'I've been wrong about you, haven't I, Georgia? All the time when I thought you were seeing your lover... That night when you never came home... You were with your aunt, weren't you?'

There was no way she could lie to him; her face had given her away before she was able to say a word.

'Why?' he demanded savagely, frightening her. 'Why didn't you say something? Why did you let me believe...?'

'It wasn't any of your business,' Georgia retaliated frantically. How much had he guessed? Not everything, surely? He had never once in the time he had been back made any reference to the night they had spent together. He probably didn't want to remember it, she had acknowledged painfully.

'Just like the child you're carrying. I suppose that isn't any of my business either, is it?'

For a moment she was too afraid, too shocked to muster any defences.

'No, it isn't. How could it be?' she lied frantically, when she could speak.

'How could it be?' The way he looked at her made her freeze with anguish. 'Do you really need to ask me that? Do I really have to spell it out for you? You and I were lovers... I thought at the time that you were using me as a substitute for someone else...that you were in some illogical way using me to fill the empty space he had left in your life...but I was wrong, wasn't I? Just as I was wrong about his being the father of your child.'

He was speaking slowly, groping for the words almost as though trying to find his way along an unfamiliar route... speaking more to himself than to her as he said half under his breath, 'Dear God, I thought at the time that you'd never...but I told myself I was wrong. Why...why in God's name did you do it?' he demanded again. 'Even when I *warned* you that I couldn't protect you from exactly this kind of consequence...'

This couldn't be happening... It was worse than even her worst imagined nightmares of how he might react to the truth. The shock in his face and voice were something that couldn't be manufactured. Georgia wanted to deny it, to tell him that he was wrong, that he wasn't the father of her child, but she knew that he wouldn't believe her.

'Why?' he asked harshly again.

'I don't really know. I think it was because of my aunt's death. I was still in shock...I...' She looked up at him and saw the way he was looking at her and tears filled her eyes. 'I didn't mean it to happen, at least not consciously... although perhaps somewhere at the back of my mind I felt that in creating a new life I was somehow compensating for my aunt's death...'

'So it wasn't *me* you wanted... just a father for your child.'

Was that relief she could hear in his voice? Why should she be so surprised if it was? She had known all along that he didn't love her... couldn't love her...

'I wasn't consciously planning to get pregnant,' she told him defensively. 'Shock does strange things to people. My aunt was...'

She couldn't go on. She could feel the full weight of her emotions welling up inside her. 'She was all I had,' she told him emotionally when she had herself back under control. 'I couldn't bear the thought of losing her. I couldn't even admit to anyone that she was dying, I was so afraid...'

'Was that why you let me think you had a lover?'

The quiet question startled her, forcing her to focus on him. She hadn't realised how much she was betraying to him, caught up in her own emotions and reliving the agony of discovering that her aunt was not after all going to recover, experiencing again her bitterness and resentment that others should be healthy and alive while her beloved aunt was dying.

She couldn't answer him, but he must have realised he had hit on the truth because his face tightened a little, and she knew he must be cursing her.

'You needn't worry that...that either I or the baby will make any claims on you,' she told him tensely. 'It wasn't your fault. As you said, you did warn me...'

'Not my *fault*...' The savagery in his voice shocked her. 'My God. Of course it's my *fault*! I should have guessed...realised...' He shook his head, and then said huskily, 'Despite all that passion, all that intensity...despite the way you touched me, somehow you were so...so untouched almost that I should have known...'

His words stunned her, bringing back instantly the full erotic awareness of how she had felt in his arms.

'We'll have to get married, of course.'

At first she thought she must have misheard him, but when she realised she had not she immediately shook her head, and said fiercely, 'No. No, I won't marry you. Not without love.'

She knew that he was looking at her, but she could not meet his eyes. If she did he was bound to see the sick longing in her own, the silent plea that he overrule the words pride had made her utter.

There was a long silence, and then he said curtly, 'I see. Well, if that's how you feel...'

How she felt... How she felt had nothing to do with what she had said. She felt as though she were slowly dying in mortal agony. She felt as though she wanted to reach out to him and cling to him physically, and to beg him never to leave her. She felt as though her world would come to an end if he left it. That was how she felt, but how could she impose her feelings on him when she knew that he didn't feel the same way about her... that he could not really want to marry her?

'People don't marry these days just because they've produced a child,' she forced herself to say. 'It was my decision to go ahead with my pregnancy. Mine, and——'

'Just as the baby is yours,' he interrupted her furiously. 'Well, I've got news for you. That baby is mine as well, and if you think for one minute that I'm going to pretend that all this hasn't happened, just because that's what *you* want...' He stopped abruptly, frowning. 'We can't discuss this now. Not while you're still so weak.' He came closer to the bed and leaned towards her, and to her astonishment he placed his hand on her belly. His touch was warm and gentle, the sensation of love and need that shot through her so strong that it made her close her eyes and tremble slightly.

'Just remember,' he told her quietly, 'this baby is mine as well as yours, and I intend to be a part of his or her life.'

'But you didn't want it. You didn't know... You can't... you thought...'

'I know now,' he told her heavily. 'I know now.'

Once he knew that the baby she was carrying was his, if anything Mitch became even more protective of her. He hadn't repeated his proposal, but he had made it very plain that he intended to be very much a part of their baby's life. To her shock he had even intimated to Louise that he was its father, causing her friend to comment, when she and Georgia were alone, that she expected she ought to have guessed.

Georgia could tell that Louise was curious about their relationship, but to her credit she made no attempt to pry or ask questions, simply accepting Georgia's unsteady comment that for a while around the time of her aunt's death she had behaved in a way that was totally out of character and that her pregnancy was the result of that behaviour.

Mitch's reaction to his discovery that he was the father of her child was so different from what she had expected that it was still difficult for her to come to terms with it. She had expected him, if he had ever found out, to reject both her and their child, but instead he was making it plain that he intended to play a very full role in their baby's life.

This morning he had gone out. He had business to attend to in London, he had told her. The midwife had called in his absence and to Georgia's delight she had told her that she was now well enough to get up.

'But only as long as you don't overdo things again,' she warned Georgia before she left her, adding with a smile, 'Mind you, somehow with Mr Fletcher around I can't see you being allowed to do that.'

Once she had gone, Georgia got up and headed for the bathroom. Half an hour later she was standing naked in front of her bedroom mirror studying her swollen body with a mixture of awe and amazement.

Engrossed in discussing with her baby the changes it had wrought on her body, she didn't realise that Mitch had returned until he opened the bedroom door and walked into her room, stopping abruptly when he saw her.

Immediately Georgia tried to reach for the dressing-gown she had left on her bed, her face going bright red with embarrassment . . . not just at her nudity but also because she was suddenly and uncomfortably aware of how unattractive she must look to Mitch, even if she herself found the changes in her body fascinating and marvellous. But even as she reached for it, Mitch stopped her, his voice thick and husky as he demanded, 'No, don't hide yourself away from me, Georgia.'

Mesmerised by the sound of his voice, the look in his eyes, Georgia stood where she was.

When his fingertips touched her skin she trembled wildly. As though it was somehow aware of what was happening, the baby kicked hard, making her gasp, causing Mitch to tense. When she saw the look in his eyes and realised that he thought she was rejecting his touch, that her gasp was caused by a revulsion against him, she reacted instinctively, catching hold of his hand and guiding it to where the baby was still kicking.

When she saw his expression change, saw the awe, the wonder . . . the love illuminating his face, her throat closed up on a huge wave of emotion.

This was how it should be; that was how she had dreamed of it being since she first knew she was carrying his child; this one moment, that one look encapsulated all her most cherished and idealistic dreams of loving and being loved, of sharing with her lover a pure and uplifting sense of togetherness and commitment to the child that was a result of their coming together.

Mitch's hand still rested on her body. The baby, quiet now, had stopped kicking. Her fingers fell away from his wrist, freeing him from her touch, but still he didn't make any attempt to move away from her.

She could feel the warmth of his body and wanted to move closer to it, to be embraced by it, to be held by it—to be held by him, she recognised as her feelings of maternal love and joy started to change to something more personal, more sensual.

Mitch's fingers stroked her skin, caressing it with slow, gentle movements that made her quiver inside and which warned her that it was time for her to move away from him . . . that, if she did not do so, she was going to betray her feelings for him and embarrass them both, spoiling the special intimacy they had just shared. But when she tried to move away he stopped her and, to her shock, knelt on the floor in front of her, and before she could stop him tenderly kissed the swollen mound of her belly.

Tears stung her eyes, so many different sensations and emotions filling her that she cried out against them, a low, tortured sound that made him lift his head and look up at her.

'This isn't going to work, is it?' he said rawly. 'I can't stay here with you like this without wanting you. I thought I could . . . I thought that just being close to you, just being able to share the baby with you would be enough, but it won't.'

His voice was flat and hard with despair and pain.

'I thought I'd experienced all the pain there was to experience when I believed you were using me as a substitute for another man...when the love and physical desire you were giving me were really meant for someone else. I thought after that that nothing could hurt me again...that it was like going through fire and being immune to it if you managed to survive the experience. Then I had to go. I couldn't stay knowing how much I loved you...how much I wanted you...how easy it would be for me to give in to the temptation to beg you to take pity on me, to tell you that the sexual chemistry between us was so strong that we could build a viable relationship on it. I was even prepared to deny my love, to jettison it completely and pretend that my need for you was only physical if in doing so I could persuade you to let me into your life. But in the end I couldn't do it. My pride wouldn't let me, and so I walked away while my pride was still strong enough to support me. I thought then that there could never be a pain like that. But I was wrong. There are other kinds of pain that are equally destructive, equally hard to bear. Like discovering how badly I'd misjudged you...how stupidly I'd allowed my parents' relationship to colour my views. To discover the truth, to discover that, while I'd been accusing *you* of trying to steal another woman's husband, you had in fact been nursing a dying woman... How you must have despised me for that. No wonder you didn't tell me the truth.

'It was Louise who did that...inadvertently, of course, not knowing just what she was telling me when she talked to me about your aunt and the strain you'd been under.

'I knew then that what my senses had been trying to tell me when we'd made love was true... that there was an innocence, an intensity about your lovemaking that...' He broke off, shaking his head.

He was, Georgia realised, trembling with emotion, and as he looked away from her and towards the window she could have sworn she had seen the damp glitter of tears in his eyes.

'Once I realised... once I knew that your child was my child...' He shook his head as though he was trying to clear his thoughts from intense emotional chaos. 'I blew it, I know, trying to pressurise you into a marriage I knew you wouldn't want. After all, if you'd cared for me at all you'd have hardly kept your pregnancy a secret from me, would you? Neither would you have let me think that you were involved with someone else. No, I know you don't love me... and foolishly I thought that just being close to you and the baby would be enough. But it isn't.'

There was anguish in the harsh sound of his voice.

'Now, seeing you like this...' He swallowed, and Georgia studied the small movement of his throat, seeing the emotional strain he was under.

'I want you so much... love you so much.' His voice was so low she could barely hear the words. 'And seeing you like this... You fill me with so much love and desire, Georgia... The reason I'm telling you all this is that I want you to understand just why I have to leave. I don't want you to think that either you or our child isn't important to me. It's just that I have to go before I do something that we'll both regret.'

He leaned forward again, his hands tracing the swell of her stomach as though he were blind, his touch so delicate, so full of love and pain that Georgia wanted to reach out and cradle him against her, to hold him and tell him how much she loved him. But, before she could do so, he was pressing his mouth to her skin, sending such sharp quivers of delight racing through her body that she cried out his name.

Instantly he released her, getting to his feet, asking her roughly, 'What is it? What have I done? Have I hurt you? Have I hurt the baby?'

Georgia couldn't speak. All she could do was to shake her head, and then, knowing that to try to explain to him all that she was feeling would take too long, would waste too much precious time, would cause them both too much anxiety, she simply held out her arms to him.

At first he didn't move, simply staring at her, his eyes so wary and confused that her heart ached for him.

This was how he must have looked as a child, torn apart by his father's unfaithfulness to his mother... initially loving both parents and not understanding what was happening... slowly realising... slowly knowing; a pain, an awareness that no child should have. Their child would never know that pain, would never have that look in the eyes she hoped would be like his father's.

'Mitch... I love you.' Her voice trembled and so did she. 'I've loved you all along. That night... the night we made love... I loved you then, even though I didn't realise it until afterwards. When I woke up and you'd gone, I thought it was because you wanted to make it plain to me that what had happened meant nothing emotionally to you.'

He still hadn't moved. He looked... he looked like a man unable to dare to allow himself to believe what he was hearing, she recognised achingly.

'Mitch, please... please hold me. I'm getting cold standing here like this. We're both getting cold,' she added huskily, patting her stomach.

If she had to be the one to go to him then she would do so, but suddenly he moved; suddenly he was there beside her, holding her, stroking her, kissing her with a hungry, fierce eagerness that made her senses thrill in response, and all the time, in between kisses, he was telling her how much he loved her... how much he wanted her... how much he desired her.

Later they made love, a slow, tender exploration of one another's bodies, culminating in a coming together that was so emotionally and physically complete that it made Georgia cry. Mitch leaned over her, carefully brushing the tears away, tenderly kissing her damp face.

'Are you sure that this is what you want... that *I'm* what you want?' he asked her huskily, and, knowing that the cause of his insecurity came from his childhood, Georgia held him lovingly and whispered truthfully,

'You are all I want, Mitch. You are all I'll ever want.'

They were married quietly three days before Christmas. On Christmas Day Mitch found Georgia in the garden, standing in front of the bare rose bushes.

'You're thinking of her, of your aunt, aren't you?' he guessed, coming to stand behind her, wrapping his arms round her and holding her tightly.

Georgia nodded. 'She would have loved you so much and been so happy for us. I just wish...' She turned in his arms and whispered huskily, 'I still miss her even now...'

'Georgia... quick, wake up!'

Muzzily Georgia opened her eyes, frowning at Mitch as she stared at the clock and saw that it was only eight o'clock.

'What is it?' she demanded urgently. 'Is Rachel...?'

'Rachel's fine... fast asleep in her cot,' Mitch assured her.

'So why did you wake me up?' Georgia grumbled. 'Saturday mornings you look after Rachel while *I* catch up on my sleep...'

Mitch was laughing at her, and her heart turned over inside her chest. She loved him so much, and since Rachel's birth four months ago he seemed at last to have put his own unhappy childhood behind him. He was a wonderful father... and an equally wonderful husband.

'Hurry up, there's something I want you to see,' he was telling her now, pushing back the bed-clothes and ignoring her protests, telling her with a smile, 'You don't need to get dressed. Just put something on your feet.'

Unwillingly Georgia followed him downstairs, blinking in the strong June sunlight as he opened the back door.

'You want me to go out into the garden? At this time on a Saturday morning? Honestly, Mitch...'

'Come on. And stop grumbling.' He ruffled her hair as he spoke, kissing the nape of her neck, sending tiny prickles of desire zinging along her spine. 'This way...'

She followed him into the garden, coming to an abrupt halt as she saw why he had woken her up and brought her out here.

There, on the bushes they had planted together, was the first of the roses, dew still on its freshly opened petals.

She was trembling as she leaned forward to breathe in its perfume, tears sparkling on her face as she turned back to Mitch and said emotionally, 'Oh, Mitch...and I was such a crosspatch. The first of Aunt May's roses...'

'I knew you would want to see it.'

As he held her and kissed her, Georgia gave a mental prayer of thankfulness for whatever strand of fate had brought him into her life. He loved her so much...understood her so well. He was her friend as well as her lover...her companion as well as her husband.

From the open bedroom window she heard Rachel's waking cry.

'Umm...sounds as if someone doesn't like missing out on anything. Shall I go up and get her or will you?' Mitch asked her.

'Let's both go...together...' Georgia suggested softly.

POSTCARDS FROM EUROPE

HARLEQUIN PRESENTS®

Travel across Europe in 1994 with Harlequin Presents. Collect a new Postcards From Europe title each month!

Don't miss
DESIGNED TO ANNOY
by Elizabeth Oldfield
Harlequin Presents #1636

Available in March wherever Harlequin Presents books are sold.

HPPFE3

Hi—

Have arrived safely in Germany, but Diether von Lössingen denies that he's the baby's father. Am determined that he shoulder his responsibilities!

Love, Sophie

P.S. Diether's shoulders are certainly wide enough.

**Fifty red-blooded, white-hot, true-blue hunks
from every State in the Union!**

Look for MEN MADE IN AMERICA! Written by some
of our most poplar authors, these stories feature fifty o
the strongest, sexiest men, each from a different state in
the union!

Two titles available every other month at your favorite
retail outlet.

In March, look for:

TANGLED LIES by Anne Stuart (Hawaii)
ROGUE'S VALLEY by Kathleen Creighton (Idaho)

In May, look for:

LOVE BY PROXY by Diana Palmer (Illinois)
POSSIBLES by Lass Small (Indiana)

You won't be able to resist MEN MADE IN AMERICA

My Valentine 1994

Celebrate the most romantic day of the year with
MY VALENTINE 1994
a collection of original stories, written by
four of Harlequin's most popular authors...

MARGOT DALTON
MURIEL JENSEN
MARISA CARROLL
KAREN YOUNG

Available in February, wherever
Harlequin Books are sold.

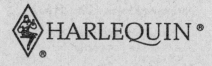

HARLEQUIN®

VAL94

When the only time you have for yourself is...

STOLEN _moments_ ™

Spring into spring—by giving yourself a March Break! Take a few _stolen moments_ and treat yourself to a Great Escape. Relax with one of our brand-new stories (or with all six!).

Each STOLEN MOMENTS title in our Great Escapes collection is a complete and never-before-published _short_ novel. These contemporary romances are 96 pages long—the perfect length for the busy woman of the nineties!

Look for Great Escapes in our Stolen Moments display this March!

SIZZLE by Jennifer Crusie
ANNIVERSARY WALTZ
by Anne Marie Duquette
MAGGIE AND HER COLONEL
by Merline Lovelace
PRAIRIE SUMMER by Alina Roberts
THE SUGAR CUP by Annie Sims
LOVE ME NOT by Barbara Stewart

Wherever Harlequin and Silhouette books are sold.

 **W🌐RLDWIDE LIBRARY** ®

Are you looking for more titles by

PENNY JORDAN

Don't miss these fabulous stories by one of
Harlequin's most renowned authors:

Harlequin Presents®

#11353	SO CLOSE AND NO CLOSER	$2.75	☐
#11369	BITTER BETRAYAL	$2.75	☐
#11388	BREAKING AWAY	$2.75	☐
#11404	UNSPOKEN DESIRE	$2.79	☐
#11418	RIVAL ATTRACTIONS	$2.79	☐
#11575	A CURE FOR LOVE	$2.99	☐
#11599	STRANGER FROM THE PAST	$2.99	☐

Harlequin® Promotional Titles

#97108	POWER PLAY	$4.95	☐
#97120	SILVER	$5.95	☐
#97121	THE HIDDEN YEARS	$5.99	☐
#97122	LINGERING SHADOWS	$5.99	☐

(limited quantities available on certain titles)

TOTAL AMOUNT	$	
POSTAGE & HANDLING	$	
($1.00 for one book, 50¢ for each additional)		
APPLICABLE TAXES*	$	_____
TOTAL PAYABLE	$	_____
(check or money order—please do not send cash)		

To order, complete this form and send it, along with a check or money order for the
total above, payable to Harlequin Books, to: *In the U.S.*: 3010 Walden Avenue,
P.O. Box 9047, Buffalo, NY 14269-9047; *In Canada*: P.O. Box 613, Fort Erie, Ontario,
L2A 5X3.

Name: _____

Address: _____ City: _____

State/Prov.: _____ Zip/Postal Code: _____

*New York residents remit applicable sales taxes.
Canadian residents remit applicable GST and provincial taxes.

HPJBACK1

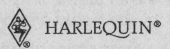

HARLEQUIN®